THE MAKESHIFT GROOM

Wrong Way Weddings Book 5

LORI WILDE &
PAM ANDREWS HANSON

D1528245

"I'm here about the wedding dress."

Jude Bailey's intercom distorted voices in strange ways, but this was the first time it had made someone sound uber sexy.

Hmm. She hadn't noticed that beguiling drawl in her visitor's voice when she'd talked to him on the phone yesterday. Maybe she'd been too eager to sell the cursed dress to notice.

Hesitating, she gnawed her bottom lip. Was it safe to just let him up? Maybe she should go to the courtyard, but that meant hauling the source of her shame—that darned wedding dress—down the stairs of her third-floor walk-up on a blustery November 4th afternoon and well...just *no.*

But she was desperate to unload the dress for some fast cash. She needed the thing out of her house and out of her mind so she could finally move on from the source of her greatest humiliation. Her ad had run for three days, and this guy was the only one who'd shown any interest.

"What's your name?" she asked, consulting the note she'd jotted down the previous day.

"Tom Brunswick."

He'd gotten that part right. Should she buzz him up or not?

"Look," he said. "I get that you're probably nervous about letting me into your apartment. That's smart. You can bring the dress down to me if that works better for you."

The fact that he offered eased her nervousness. Quickly, she texted her cousin Leigh and told her what the situation was, just to be safe. Although she wasn't sure how much help Leigh could be, living in another country.

"It's a big dress and a three-story walk-up. I'll buzz you in." She pushed the button to let him into the vestibule, opened her door a crack with the chain on, and waited for him to climb the stairs to her apartment.

While she waited, she mused. What kind of man bought a wedding dress for his fiancée? What kind of bride would go along with that? It sounded a bit controlling. Just like Jaxon.

At the thought of her ex, she cringed.

Forget Jaxon. You're better off without him.

Yes, she understood she'd dodged a bullet, but getting stood up at the church in front of a hundred guests could do a number on a woman's self-confidence.

She shook her spine. *Head in the game.*

If Tom Brunswick was bargain hunting, he'd come to the right place. Like her Craig's List ad said, she was open to all offers, whatever it took to get the wretched thing out of her closet.

From her vantage point, she could see the top of his head with his dark-brown hair, brushed back off his forehead and just long enough to appear unruly in a sexy way.

An instant later, he climbed the last step and any resemblance to a shaggy dog ended at his hairline. He was a genuine hunk, six feet of muscle and sex appeal packed into a worn brown leather bomber jacket and tight faded jeans.

Whoa! A warm tingle lit up her stomach. It had been a while since she'd noticed men in that way, and it felt good to have blood flow in her lower regions again.

"You're Jude?" He glanced at his phone. "Jude Bailey?"

"Yes."

He raised his head and his gaze. His eyes landed on hers and he offered up a charming grin. "Any kin to the Bailey Baby Products Baileys?"

"Distant cousins," she said.

She might be descended from the same great grandparents as the wealthy Baileys, and her cousin Leigh had literally married into royalty, but Jude's branch of the family hadn't inherited the money-making—or apparently—the good-matchmaking gene. Her own parents had been married for forty years so she had that going for her.

Although her folks had moved to Florida last year when Dad retired. Her older brother Mike was happily married to his high school sweetheart and they had a new baby girl. Everyone in her family had found someone to share their lives with. Why couldn't she?

And even though she had lots of friends, sometimes Jude felt lonely not having family close by.

"Do you want to bring the dress into the hall-way?" The stranger eyed her through the door crack.

"Oh, no, sorry." Why did gorgeous men always make her act like a total dodo? "Just let me take the chain off."

She unintentionally slammed the door in his face with a loud bang, then fumbled with the chain and opened it again, relieved that he was still standing there. "Come in. The dress is right here on the couch."

Waving him into the room, she left the door wide open...just to be safe.

He stepped into the living room and slowly appraised her from where she hovered in the entryway. "You look about right."

"What?" She eyed the hallway in case she needed to run or scream and kept her cell phone in her hand.

"For the dress."

"Huh?" She closed one eye and canted her head, hoping a different angle would help her make more sense of what he was saying. Was he being weird?

He gave her the once-over, from the top of her head to her feet and back up again.

Jude imagined his dark-brown laser eyes dissolving her clothes. Oops. That was not what she should be thinking.

"The size."

Oh. Not a weirdo after all. "As I said in the ad, it's a size six."

"Same size as Tara, but I wanted to make sure." He looked from Jude to the dress that she'd artfully fanned out over the back of the couch.

"Tara is your fiancée?"

"My sister is the bride," he said. "You thought I was buying a used wedding dress for my fiancée?"

"No, no." Yes. But if his sister was the bride, why was he buying the dress?

"Tara is my twin actually." He rubbed his hands on the sides of his jeans, then lifted one sleeve of the gown, seemingly checking the length without touching the beaded bodice. "She's a little taller than you, but this should still work."

"Why did your sister send you to buy her wedding dress?" Jude asked, unable to contain her curiosity.

"This is a last-minute replacement. Tara had a dress being altered, but there was a fire at the bridal shop. Heavy smoke and water damage. The shop will refund her money, but not until the insurance pays out which will be weeks. In the meantime, she needs an affordable alternative."

"How terrible for her," Jude murmured, unable to tell whether he approved of the dress or not. "It's really nice of you to help her find a replacement. When's the wedding?"

"This Saturday."

"Wow, just three days away. She must be desperate, but why she'd send you? Doesn't she want to see the dress for herself?"

"I showed her the pics you posted in your online ad, and she gave me a thumbs-up to buy it if it's in as good a shape as the ad said it is. Tara's a pilot and she's grounded in Salt Lake until the freak late season snowstorm there abates. She'll get here in time for the wedding, but not in time to shop for a new dress."

"She must be frantic, trying to get home for the wedding, and she doesn't even have a gown." Jude tried to imagine a female version of Tom with his dark bedroom eyes, rumpled dark hair, and dynamite good looks.

"You said the dress has never been worn?"

"No—I mean yes, that's what I said. It's brand new. I couldn't take it back because there's no return on wedding gowns."

"You were going to wear it?"

"Yes."

"But you didn't."

"No." She swallowed back a sigh. "Things didn't work out."

"I hate to hear that."

"It was for the best." She forced a smile.

"What happened?" His tone made it clear he was just being polite and didn't really care that she'd gotten jilted on her wedding day, but his question still bothered her. She wasn't past the hurt yet.

"Yes, apparently at the last minute my ex decided he preferred a stock car racer to a quiet bookworm."

"Ouch," Tom said. "That sucks."

Yes, indeed. "He also said I was boring."

"Hey, I'm sorry." He probably meant he was sorry he'd asked.

"It was six months ago. I'm over it." For the most part, she *was* over Jaxon, but she wasn't over the "boring" comment. "Of course, my parents had to pay for the reception hall they'd rented, and my aunt Ellen doesn't know what to do with the four pounds of hand-molded pastel mints in her freezer. Does your sister need any candy wedding bells?"

"Uh, no, thanks." He looked like he wanted to get out of there ASAP. "About the dress—are you sure you want to sell it? I mean, a nice person like you, I'm sure you'll get a chance to wear it eventually."

Nice. That cursed word again.

"I need the closet space." She didn't tell him how fervently she wanted to get it out of her apartment, out of the suburb of Roseville, and preferably out of the state of Illinois. Start over somewhere new and exciting.

"I can understand that." He glanced around at the tiny one-bedroom apartment.

"Why did you call me a 'nice' person?"

"Well..." He averted his gaze, pretending to study the voluminous skirt of the wedding dress. "You do seem nice."

Something inside her snapped. He was a stranger.

She had nothing whatsoever to lose by asking him The Big Question. So she asked.

"I *am* nice, really nice, so why don't hot guys like *you* want to marry nice women like *me*?"

He raised his arms in a gesture of surrender. "Miss —Jude, I don't know you well enough to—"

She leaned in. "No, I really want to know. What's wrong with being nice?"

"Just because some jerk broke up with you—"

"He dumped me at the church when I was about to put on the dress, and then he tried to tell me I'm too good for him." Why was she telling him all this? *Zip your lip, Bailey.*

"Look." He raised his palms. "I had no idea what was in that guy's head, but there's nice, and then there's being a doormat. Maybe that's the real problem. Do you let people walk all over you?"

"I'm not a doormat." Was she?

He shrugged and lifted the other lacy sleeve of the gown. "I think Tara will like this."

"Fine. You can have the dress for three hundred less than I paid for it. I can show you the receipt, but *only* if you tell me what's wrong with being nice. I bet you've broken up with women and used the same lame excuse that she was too good for you. Or that she's too sweet. Or you just wanted to be friends."

"I don't think I've ever said *that*...exactly." He ran

a finger around his collar and glanced at the front door. "But let me just text Tara to see if the dress will do."

"Go right ahead." Jude flapped a hand. "I can wait."

WHEW, BOY.

Jude Bailey might be cute as the dickens, but right now, holding his feet to the fire the way she was, she didn't seem all that "nice" to Tom.

He texted Tara a picture of the dress—and told her Jude's sob story and why the brand-new bridal gown was so cheap—but his twin didn't answer right away.

Darn it. He wanted to grab that dress and get out of there.

That left an awkward silence between them as Jude stood near the open door, her phone in her hand as if she intended on calling 911 at the slightest provocation.

Message received. She was the cautious type and she didn't trust him. Not that he could blame her. He was a stranger, and she was home alone.

"Could I see the receipt?" he asked just to make

sure he was getting the dress at the discount she offered.

"First," she said. "Answer my question."

Tom grimaced. It wasn't an easy question to answer. She'd hit a sore spot. He'd used precisely those same words just days ago to break up with a cute, but marriage-minded redhead he'd been seeing for a couple of weeks.

He wasn't the love-'em-and-leave-'em type. He just enjoyed his freedom too much to settle down right now. His handcrafted furniture store was finally a success, and he wanted to bask in that glow for a while.

And then there was the ridiculous no-sex bar bet he'd made with his best buddies just last night—Jake, Dirk, and Seth. For the first time since they'd met in their frat house at the University of Illinois, all four of them were flying solo at the same time.

After a basketball game that Tom and Seth won, they ended up at a trendy nightclub lamenting their trouble with women. The drunken conversation had devolved into a celibacy challenge along the lines of their favorite frat house classic movie—*40 Days and 40 Nights*.

At some point, Dirk, a day trader, slapped three hundred dollars on the middle of the pool table and ponied up a bet that sent the rest of them running to the ATM.

"Forty day and forty nights, lads," Dirk said in a horrible imitation of an Irish accent. "Twelve hundred dollars up for grabs. No sex for forty days and that includes refraining from... er...shall we say...*self-care*. Whoever lasts the longest wins the pot."

They'd done a similar challenge in their college days, and Tom had lost on the thirty-ninth day when a waitress he'd been crushing on slipped him her phone number. As it turned out, Dirk had put her up to the seduction, leaving Tom feeling cheap and used.

Dirk hadn't let him forget it either. For ten years he'd been bragging about besting Tom, who was easily the most competitive of their group and had gotten his head turned by a sexy wiggle and soft giggle.

This time, Tom was determined to win that bet and put an end to Dirk's gloating once and for all.

"Well?" Jude asked, fixing him with her intelligent blue eyes.

Tom blinked, momentarily lost in thought. "Huh?"

"What's wrong with being nice?"

"Um, it's not the niceness per se."

"No?" She didn't look as if she was buying it.

"Sometimes, the chemistry just isn't there. Or

maybe the timing is wrong." He shrugged, wishing she'd let the whole thing go.

"Bad chemistry." She wrinkled her pert little nose and stared at him. "Next you'll tell me men do like *nice* women—but only as pals."

He shifted from one foot to the other, torn between wanting to cheer her up and yearning to escape because those rosy lips puckered into a kiss-able *O* where doing him in and thirty-nine days stood between him and twelve hundred dollars and the title of sole survivor.

"About the dress—"

"I'm sick of being a nice woman and getting dumped for it. I'm changing my image," she declared.

"You've been dumped more than once?"

She made a face that he took as a *yes*.

Umm, okay. It seemed he'd walked in on her struggling with some emotional demons. Not really his circus or his monkeys. Her shoulders slumped, and he was afraid she'd start crying. He should have known there was some kind of emotional injury behind a never-worn wedding dress.

Jude wrung her hands. "I *want* to change. I just don't have a clue where to start."

Why was she asking him for advice? What did he know about committed relationships? His self-preservation instincts told him to leave it alone, but her big baby-blues reeled him in. She needed help.

Boy, did she need help!

What the heck? Advice was free. Right?

"You don't need to change your personality. Just your attitude."

"Excuse me?" That seemed to tick her off. Her eyes narrowed and her lips pursed, and she looked quite fierce. There was spunk in this woman, and she didn't even seem to know it.

He had one foot in quicksand. It was definitely time to fall back and regroup. Jude Bailey was gorgeous. Long, dark, silky hair. Luscious curves that couldn't be concealed by her jeans and a bulky red sweatshirt. An adorable round face with a sexy mouth and big blue doe eyes.

"You're cute. You come across as open, caring..." He nearly said *nice*. "What you need to consider is that men like a bit of mystery. Be more aloof. Casual. Act like you don't care."

And don't ask strangers for lovelorn advice, he wanted to add.

"My mother told me all that when I first started dating, but you make it sound like you're leaking tribal secrets. I'm as aloof as the next woman."

If she was aloof, he was the Abominable Snowman. In fact, everything he'd seen so far showed she was just the opposite: forthright, sweet, vulnerable—a very nice woman. One a guy could take home to meet his parents. Exactly the sort of woman he *wasn't* looking for. Especially now. He had twelve hundred dollars to win and a decade of ribbing to end.

"It's the best I can offer," he said. "When the chemistry is right with a guy, you'll know it. Trust your gut."

She sighed. "I almost flunked freshman chemistry in college, so there's that. Do you want the dress or not?"

"Yeah, it's nice. I'm pretty sure my sister will want it, but she hasn't texted me back yet. Could you possibly hold it until tomorrow?"

Jude shrugged. "Sure, why not?"

"Hey, cheer up, there's a lot to be said for not getting married young. You're only—what? Twenty-one?"

"Twenty-six."

Really? That surprised him. She looked much younger.

"Still a kid." He grinned, but she didn't grin back. "I just hit the big three-oh myself and I'm light-years away from taking the big step."

"I'll hold the dress until you check with your sister. If the price is a problem—"

"No, the price is fine." He'd be embarrassed to buy it for any less. It was a beautiful wedding dress.

She walked him to the door, then closed and locked it behind him.

"I'll tell you what's wrong with nice women," he muttered under his breath. "They make guys feel like jerks in comparison."

2

Later that night, Tara called him, and her first few words told him how edgy she was. The sooner this wedding business was over, the happier he'd be.

"Describe the dress to me," his sister said. "Is it pure white or ivory?"

"It looked white to me. There are little beads on top."

"Pearls? What about lace? It isn't too fussy, is it?"

"It's pretty and it's never been worn. The woman who's selling it was jilted on her wedding day."

"Eww."

"What does that mean?"

"Do you think the dress is jinxed?"

"Woman, you're a pilot. Don't be superstitious."

"You're right. Being snowed in is playing havoc with my nerves."

"Ben loves you," Tom reassured her. "It's going to be fine."

"I don't know about that. First a fire in the bridal shop, then getting snowed in—"

"Nerves are understandable."

"What's she like?"

"Who?"

"The woman who got dumped at the altar."

"Cute, petite," Tom said without hesitation, remembering just how gorgeous Jude was, then added, "Nice."

"So not your type at all. You go for the tall drop-dead knockouts that treat you with indifferent disdain."

"That's not true."

"Amanda. Need I say more?"

"You don't even need to say that."

Tara shifted gears, thankfully leaving her criticism of his choice in girlfriends. "What if this woman sells the dress to someone else? Tom, why didn't you just buy it? You know I'm desperate!"

"Don't worry. She's holding it for me."

"Oh, sure. If she gets a better offer, she'll turn it down just in case you decide to buy it. Be real. Not even you have that much sway over a stranger. Did you at least give her a deposit?"

"Never thought of it."

He tried to be tolerant of Tara's prewedding jitters, but he could feel his neck muscles tensing. He'd never tell her—and he hated admitting it to himself—but he wouldn't mind going back for another look at Jude Bailey.

What for? You've got a bet to win. No sex for the next thirty-nine days.

"Buy the dress, Tom," Tara insisted. "I can't get married without a wedding gown. Go get it tomorrow and please don't blow this."

"I'm on it, I'm on it."

"Everything needs to be perfect," Tara said. "By the way, have you found a date for the wedding?"

"Not yet."

"Well, get on it, will you, and this time, could you bring someone nice?"

"I can't come stag?"

"You'll mess up the seating arrangement."

"Can't have that, can we?"

"Please," she whispered. "I'm hanging by a thread here as I stand at the window, watching the snow coming down."

"Got you covered, sis. I won't let you down. I'll

find someone to sit next to me at your wedding. Even if it's a total stranger."

EARLY THE NEXT MORNING, TOM CALLED JUDE after he arrived at his store. He breathed in the smell of sawdust and smiled. He loved his shop. Loved carving furniture and making something of quality that would last a lifetime in this throwaway world.

"My sister wants the dress," he told Jude. "I can come over anytime today. I own my own business so I can rearrange my schedule as I like."

"I'm in the car headed to work and I had to pull over to take your call. So I need to make this quick. Drop by after school, say fiveish?"

"School? You're a teacher?"

"Librarian at Evergreen High School."

That didn't surprise him. From all the bookshelves he'd seen in her living room, the career choice fit.

"No librarian jokes," she said.

"I wasn't thinking of any."

"Oh."

"Your apartment is on my route home. I'll be there at five."

"See you then."

AT ONE MINUTE AFTER FIVE HE BUZZED HER apartment and identified himself. This time she let him in without hesitating.

Her cheeks were pink, as though she'd just rushed in from the cold, and she seemed a little breathless.

"I left the dress out in case you wanted another look," she said, leading him to the couch in the cozy living room done in shades of bright yellow and muted green. The end tables that she'd painted a nice sage green resembled raw tables he carried in the store.

"Nice tables," he said, wondering why he hadn't noticed them the first time he'd been here. Probably because he'd been too busy scoping out Jude's firm little butt.

"Thanks. I bought them unfinished and painted them myself."

"Did you get them from the Artisan Gallery on Euclid?"

"Yes." Her eyes rounded in surprise. "How did you know?"

"That's my store."

"No kidding?" She looked impressed. "It's a terrific store. Awesome selection. Unique products."

"Thanks." He nodded at the end tables. "You did

a good job with the painting. A lot of people just slap on paint without sanding or priming first, and then they wonder why it looks shoddy."

Why was he talking about this? None of it had anything to do with getting a dress for his sister. It was dumb to feel so darned pleased because Jude had bought a couple of his end tables, but dang it, he was flattered.

"I guess you bought them from one of my clerks," he added, wondering how he could have possibly forgotten someone as attractive as Jude. "I don't remember you."

"It was an older woman," she said. "With a bubbly personality."

"My mother helps out sometimes when she needs mad money."

"She was very helpful." Jude grinned wide.

He canted his head. "Is something funny?"

She tapped her bottom lip with an index finger. "I probably shouldn't tell you."

Wondering what stunt his gregarious mother had pulled, Tom shook his head "Nothing Mom does surprises me."

She giggled self-consciously. "She mentioned something about wishing her son would find a *nice* woman. She complained that his 'girlfriend picker' was broken."

He groaned.

"I shouldn't have told you," she said. "It was small talk. I mentioned I wanted the tables for a new apartment after I got dumped—"

"About the dress..." He wasn't going to give her a chance to reminisce about the wedding that wasn't. It was time she moved on. "I have cash."

"Great. I'll put the gown in the garment bag it came in."

"That'd be nice—er—good, thanks."

She disappeared into the bedroom and returned with a transparent garment bag and a padded satin hanger, and then Jude looked around as though she'd lost something.

"Is there a problem?"

"No, I'm just deciding how to do this without wrinkling the dress."

"Can I help? I'm pretty good at getting big things into tight spaces." Belatedly, he realized how that sounded, and it was his turn to blush. "I was talking about furniture—you know, packing a lot of product into the delivery van."

"Uh-huh," she said dryly.

Ducking his head to hide his flushed cheeks, he said, "Here, give me the bag, and you get the dress. If we do it on the bed, everything will be fine."

Inwardly, Tom groaned. Had he actually just said

that?

"Fine?" She seemed puzzled.

He kept digging himself in deeper. "I mean, that way the dress won't drag on the floor."

"Oh, okay." She picked up the voluminous dress, folded it over her arm, and led the way to her bedroom.

Once there, Tom spread the bag on her quilted patchwork bedspread and pulled open the zipper, trying not to inhale the teasingly feminine fragrance of the room. She had good taste in scented candles, if that was what he was smelling.

The bed was full size, and they nearly bumped heads when they both bent over to ease the gown into the bag.

"Don't let the skirt catch in the zipper," she warned.

"I'll let you handle the zipper." He straightened and watched the top of her head as she carefully zipped the bag closed.

"There." She straightened and stared at the dress with forlorn nostalgia.

That look did something to him. She'd been through a lot, and he felt a surprising kick of sympathy. To her, the dress must represent lost hope.

"Hey," he said. "Why don't you come to the wedding with me?"

Huh? Where in the heck had *that* come from? Tom clenched his jaw and prayed she hadn't heard him.

She blinked. "To your sister's wedding?"

"It might be good for you."

"Good for me?"

"You know, face the trauma head-on."

She made a face.

"Besides," he said. "I need a date. My sister is as anxious as a cat on a hot tin roof and she says if I don't have a date it will mess up her seating chart. I'm trying to keep her freak-outs to a minimum."

"You waited until the last minute to find a date?"

"Well, no. I had a date, but we broke up." *C'mon, lady, just say no. I goofed when I made the invitation.*

"I see."

"There will be lot of single guys there. You might meet someone." *Shut up, Brunswick. Stop trying to sell it.*

"So might you. Wouldn't it be better for you to go alone?"

Yes, well, that was the thing. He'd made this stupid bar bet and while it might be immature of him to let competition get the better of him, he was determined to best Dirk this time. Having a date that wasn't really a date would keep other women at bay, which was the point.

He made a big show of gathering up the dress,

deeply regretting his impulsive invitation and expecting her to turn him down. The last thing a jilted bride wanted was to watch someone else get married in *her* gown. Right?

She paused, studying him, and then stunned him by shrugging and saying, "Sure, why not? I survived my cousin's wedding last month, and no one at your sister's will be whispering 'Poor Jude' behind my back."

The woman made it sound as much fun as a root canal, but he didn't see any way to renege. Besides, a wedding might be just what she needed to get out of her slump—although he didn't have a clue why he should care.

"If you're sure," he said, giving her a chance to back out.

"Unless you want to change your mind?"

"No, not at all. You'll be helping me out. My mother has her three sisters dedicated to finding a *nice* woman for me. You'll be doing me a huge favor."

"Um..."

"Yes?" His eyes met hers.

"There is *one* thing."

"What's that?"

She headed for the living room and he followed, pulling the envelope of cash from his jacket pocket. "For the dress."

"Thank you. I don't quite know how to ask this but—"

"Straight-out works for me. Spill it."

"I was wondering, while we're at the wedding, if you could watch me in action and give me a few pointers on what I'm doing wrong?" She was blushing so furiously he didn't have the heart to make a joke of it. She was serious about this.

"Look, I'm really the wrong person to ask. It's not like I'm a relationship whiz or anything." In fact, he hadn't been in a long-term relationship since well, college.

"Think of it as tutoring. I'm tired of being Miss Goody Two-Shoes and want to cut loose and enjoy myself, but I really don't know how."

"Don't you have girlfriends you could ask to teach you how not to be nice?"

"They tell me I'm perfect the way I am, but I'm not."

"You're being awfully hard on yourself."

"I just feel stagnant being a Goody Two-Shoes. It's hampering my growth as a person."

"Goody Two-Shoes?"

"It's an inside joke. My brother used to call me that because I never got into trouble and now, I feel like I have that sign around my neck that says, *take advantage of me*."

Tom shook his head. "Maybe attending the wedding as my date isn't such a good idea after all."

"You're uninviting me?"

"No, but if you're having second thoughts, I get it." He was the one who should be wearing a sign. A *Kick Me* placard.

"So you won't help me?" A shadow of sadness clouded up her eyes.

"Okay, I'll give it a shot."

"I'm thinking of a business arrangement—an exchange. My ex-fiancé gave me two season passes to the Bulls games as an engagement present."

"Do you love the Bulls?"

"No."

"Then why did he give you season passes?"

She shrugged. "I'm starting to realize he didn't really pay much attention to what I liked. Of course, he intended to use one of the seats himself, but so far, he hasn't had enough nerve to ask me to return them. You don't have to guarantee results. Just give me some advice on how I can be a little bolder, a little less 'nice,' and the tickets are yours."

Tom felt slightly panicky. "I'm more than willing to buy them from you."

"They're not for sale."

"You're willing to give them to me in exchange for dating advice, but you won't sell them. That's whack."

"I'm desperate."

"Desperate?" he echoed.

"I feel like I'm stuck in a mud bog while everyone around me zooms on by with their life. Please help me?"

Lord, she looked so beguiling. Plus, Bulls season tickets!

He couldn't hold back a grin. Season tickets in exchange for showing her how to cut loose and have fun? Why not?

"This is the craziest deal I've ever been offered," he said.

"Does that mean you'll do it?" She looked so hopeful with her wide blue eyes and earnest smile that he couldn't resist.

"I can't make any promises. I may not be much help."

"Maybe not, but if my ex-fiancé gets up enough courage to ask for the tickets back, I'd love to tell him what I did with them."

He took a deep breath. She deserved a bit of sweet revenge. He liked her more, knowing she wasn't quite so nice. See? He had something to work with.

"Lady," Tom said and stuck out his hand. "You've got a deal."

3

"I'd love to do a Zoom call with you tomorrow to see your new house, but I have plans," Jude said on Friday afternoon, her cell phone tucked underneath her chin as she shelved books after the last class of the day had left the library.

"Plans?" her cousin Leigh asked. "Do you have a date?"

"Sort of, but not really."

"Did you meet someone? Have you been holding out? Deets. I need deets."

"It's not a real a date. I'm just attending a wedding."

"Wedding?" Leigh, the woman who'd gotten married in a palace, squealed. "Why didn't you say so? Who's getting married?"

The phone slipped from under her chin, but she

managed to catch it before it hit the floor. Any other time she'd be eager to tell Leigh about her date, but how could she explain Tom Brunswick and the weird bargain they'd struck?

"A female pilot named Tara is getting married. That's all I know."

"You're attending the wedding of someone you don't know? Are you crashing the wedding?"

"No, I'm the last-minute date for the woman's twin brother, Tom, so that he doesn't have to go alone."

"Jude, that's great! I'm so excited for you. Even if this date doesn't lead to anything, it's high time you got out of that apartment—"

"It won't lead to anything. We're doing each other a favor. Quid pro quo."

"Still, that sounds like it could have possibilities. Is he cute?"

"Very."

"Woo-hoo. I want to hear *everything*."

"If I get home early enough from the wedding, I'll call and tell you how it went," Jude promised.

"Remember I'm six hours ahead. Call me no matter how late it is your time," Leigh said. "Unless things get hot and heavy with you two. In which case call me on Sunday."

"Things *won't* get hot and heavy."

"Not if you say it won't. Think positive! Open yourself up to possibilities."

"Talk to you later." Her palm was sweaty as she slipped the phone into her pocket and shelved a Stephen King novel. She focused on filing the books as efficiently as possible, but before she could finish shelving the stack of books on her rolling cart, her cell phone buzzed again.

Tom Brunswick.

Dude, just text. His voice was way too sexy. She didn't want to hear it when she was already so nervous. Then another thought occurred to her, *he's calling to cancel; that's why he didn't just text.*

She answered the phone with, "If you've changed your mind, I totally get it."

"No way! We have a deal. I just wanted to check in and see if there was anything you needed me to pick up for you before I head your way tomorrow."

Aww, that was sweet.

She shouldn't get sappy over the guy. He wasn't for her.

Why not? asked a voice at the back of her mind. *Why not have a little fun?*

Oops, that was a dangerous thought.

"Tom, I don't think we should do this—" Suddenly, she felt in over her head.

"It'll be all right," he soothed in that throaty voice

of his. "I'm off to the rehearsal dinner and then the bachelor party after that. I'll see you at tomorrow at two thirty."

And then he ended the call.

Right on the dot, Tom climbed the stairs to Jude's apartment, wondering if the barbaric rite of the bachelor party was worth his aching head and cottony mouth. The dress shoes squeaked and pinched his toes. He'd swear they weren't the ones he'd tried on a couple of weeks ago at the tux shop.

The light at the end of the tunnel was Jude.

He couldn't wait to see her again.

And that was bad.

One of his three buddies was already out of the challenge. Seth texted Tom that morning to say he'd hooked up the exotic dancer from the bachelor party and well, *c'est la vie*.

Tom was *determined* to win the bet against Dirk and put an end to a decade of teasing. Maybe he could make an excuse to Jude. She's already told him it was okay to have second thoughts.

But no, she would be dressed up and waiting. No way would he stand her up on such short notice. Not after what she'd been through.

Think about basketball, he told himself. Nothing like a ball soaring through the air for a clean three-pointer. How hard could it be to keep things light and casual between them? Just two new acquaintances going to a wedding together.

Oh, crap, that sounded like romcom.

Bail out, Brunswick, while you still can!

Somewhere in the great urban sprawl of Chicago there had to be another pair of Bulls tickets, and for the first time since starting his business, he could afford to pay top dollar if need be. He didn't have to go through with this deal he'd made. He wasn't responsible for Jude's love life.

The door inched open, and he was unprepared for what he saw.

Jude was a total knockout. Skimpy little black dress that showed off her shapely thighs and fit snugly in all the right places, accentuating her lush curves. She had on four-inch stilettos and modest gold jewelry. Understated but elegant. A feast for the eyes.

His mouth watered, and his body tightened, and oh, he was in so much trouble. "Holy smokes! You're a knockout!"

Her cheeks pinked. "Thank you. It's nice of you to say."

"I wasn't trying to be nice. That dress is great."

And so was the body poured into it. Suddenly his head wasn't the only thing throbbing. "Can I have a glass of water and a couple of aspirins? Too much bachelor party last night."

"Is ibuprofen okay?"

"Fine, thanks."

She put on her coat while he stood by the sink in her little kitchen and swallowed a couple of pills. Her navy wool coat had a belt on the back and a plaid scarf was tucked under the collar—exactly what he'd expect her to wear: sensible.

But the dress *was* something else. Had she bought it for the occasion?

"Ready?" he asked.

"I'm a little nervous," she admitted, and he found her vulnerability touching. "I'm second-guessing this whole being bold thing."

Me too. She needed a bodyguard in that dress.

"I thought we had a deal," he said. "I give you tips on what you're doing that's causing guys to pass you by and I get Bulls tickets."

"Yes, here, take the tickets." She handed him a plain white envelope, but he gave it back.

"I'll buy them, or I'll earn them. You can't just give them to me."

"Why not?"

"Leave them here and come to the wedding. We'll

see how things work out, but I'm having a hard time believing you need advice from me."

"Okay." She turned to put the tickets in the desk drawer.

Whatever he'd been drinking last night had given him X-ray vision, because when she returned, he could still see her in that little black dress, even with the coat buttoned all the way up to her chin.

❦

AT THE CHURCH A SHORT WHILE LATER, TOM took his position as an usher and left Jude on her own to kill time until the ceremony started.

She signed the guest book under the welcoming eye of its busty blond keeper, made an unnecessary trip to the restroom to futz with her makeup, and loitered in the rectory hall, looking at Sunday school rooms through the windows of locked doors and reading notices on the bulletin board about potluck suppers, prayer vigils, and charity drives.

Feeling more self-conscious with each passing minute, she started looking for the back exit, but Tom waylaid her and insisted on ushering her to one of the choice aisle seats just behind those reserved for the relatives of the bride.

"Don't you want to take your coat off?" he asked. "I'll hang it up for you."

"It's chilly in here."

"Worried that you look too hot in that dress?" he teased.

"No," she denied. *Yes.* Jude sat red-faced, thinking of all the clever quips she should have made.

Guests began arriving in droves, and the perfumed air around her warmed as the rows filled. She unbuttoned her coat, then slipped her arms out to free her movement, but kept it wrapped around her shoulders.

She couldn't bring herself to sit there baring a shoulder. She wasn't cut out to be a bold, devil-may-care woman. She was only staying because leaving would be too conspicuous—that and Tom was blocking the exit. He seemed determined to earn those Bulls tickets—even if she'd changed her mind about wanting his advice.

The processional started. A little flower girl in a pale-peach dress conscientiously dropped white rose petals, followed by a bevy of bridesmaids in high-waisted, narrow-skirted sage-green gowns.

Jude had to give the bride high marks on her choice of bridesmaid dresses, but she dreaded the reception even more now. She'd never seen so many slender, gorgeous bridesmaids in one wedding. Her black dress was going to stand out in the crowd when she desperately wanted to blend in. She didn't want to take any attention away from the bride.

Everyone stood up when the bride started down the aisle, and all eyes turned to watch her. It suddenly hit Jude like a fist to the solar plexus. Tom's twin sister was wearing *her* wedding dress.

The dress was perfect. Not gaudy or overdone. A dream of a dress with a delicately beaded satin bodice hugging the bride's breasts and waist and a skirt that floated along on the white carpet runner like a shimmering cloud.

She closed her eyes, suddenly hating the idea of a stranger in her gown.

Coward.

Fine, okay, she'd watch.

She'd gone to a dozen shops to find the perfect bridal gown, and she should have been wearing it and coming down the aisle on her father's arm. The thought of her disastrous wedding day had Jude taking a deep, calming breath.

Jude's eyes misted, and she forced herself to look at the bride's face, a feminine version of Tom's good looks. Tara was striking, not surprising since her twin brother was the handsomest man Jude had ever met. She must have been crazy—and a little desperate—to ask him to help her cut loose and have fun at the wedding.

Quickly, she cast a glance at Tom who was standing at the front of the church beside the groom and his best man and her heart skipped a beat.

Whatever had made her think he'd want to play Henry Higgins to her Eliza Doolittle? When this was over—and it would be as soon as she could get an Uber and make her escape—she'd mail him the tickets with an apology for intruding on his sister's wedding and thank him for being so gracious.

The groom was good-looking too—no surprise—but he was either hungover from the bachelor party too or scared out of his wits because his face was pale and wan under waves of coal-black hair, but when he stepped forward and smiled at his bride, his entire face lit up.

Aww!

Now that she thought about it, Jaxon had never looked at *her* that way. To her surprise and relief, she didn't much care anymore. Jaxon had loved Jaxon and she hadn't seen it. The therapist she'd seen after the failed wedding said she hadn't been able to spot Jaxon's narcissistic tendencies because she'd been projecting her goodness and kind intentions onto him and that led her to make excuses whenever a small red flag popped up.

Truly, she'd had a narrow escape, and she was grateful he'd dumped her. She'd cast Jaxon in the role of her true love because she'd desperately wanted one special person in her life, but he'd blown it.

Him, not her. Yes, she'd made a mistake in falling for his initial charm, but she knew better now, and that education was priceless.

Attending this wedding was shock therapy. Watching another woman get married in her dress was crushing, but it stirred up constructive anger. She *was* a good person, and she hadn't deserved to be jilted on her wedding day.

She let the coat slide off her shoulders. No more sitting home feeling sorry for herself! She was turning the page, starting a new chapter.

Bold and brave, here I come.

After the ceremony, the newlyweds rushed down the aisle, beaming at each other, while the ushers remained behind to dismiss the guests row by row. Tom was standing at her side, smiling and having conversations with people as they left the church.

Some men looked stiff and uncomfortable in tuxes, but Tom seemed totally at ease in the black formal wear, stiff white shirt, bow tie, and red rosebud boutonniere. His tousled dark-brown hair curled over the collar of the jacket in back and spilled over his forehead, softening the thrust of high cheek-bones and a strong chin.

He was something straight out of a wedding magazine fantasy.

She was close enough now so she couldn't see his face without looking up, but the part of him at eye level gave her shivers. His stomach was flat and his fine-tuned muscular body shoved her imagination into overdrive.

"You look great," he whispered, his mouth so close to her ear she could feel a warm tickle of air. "I'm glad you took your coat off."

Feeling self-conscious by his frank admiration, she pulled her coat back on as she joined the crowd flowing down the aisle to the receiving line near the outer door. Shy about introducing herself to the bride wearing her dress with so many other people around, Jude found a deserted spot beside the guest book stand to wait for a lull in the action so she could meet Tara.

"You're with Tom?" The well-endowed blonde who'd manned the book studied her with a surprised stare.

"Yes, I am," she said, surprised herself by the swell of pride in her chest. Any urge she had to explain the real nature of their relationship vanished in the competitive glare coming from behind excessively long eyelash extensions.

So much for making new friends.

When Tom found her, he linked his arm through hers and escorted her over to meet Tara and her new husband, Ben, who was a pastry chef. The moment wasn't as awkward as Jude feared.

Tara gushed over the dress and told Jude how honored she was that she'd come to the wedding. Tom's sister was smart and lively, and Jude found herself wishing she could get to know Tara better. They chitchatted for a few minutes, but then the photographer showed up to whisk the wedding party to the front lawn.

Jude watched from afar, enjoying seeing Tom interact with his family.

When the picture-taking was over, she rode alone with Tom to the reception. She couldn't help feeling like she was intruding and wondered why she'd *really* come. After digging around in her psyche for an answer, this was all she could come up with.

Tom was hot and she was lonely.

Thankfully, the trip to the reception hall was short, and they kept up a casual conversation about the ceremony, but that was as deep as it went.

Inside the large squat building rented out for the reception, Tom led her to the coat check desk and scanned the crowd through the double doors of the main room where a three-piece band was tuning up.

She unbuttoned her coat.

Tom was behind her, helping her out of it before she could do it herself. When his fingers brushed against her bare shoulder, Jude tingled all the way to her tailbone.

"Tom, honey, save a dance for me." A tall, honey-haired bridesmaid wiggled her fingers at him as she passed.

Jude recognized her as the bridesmaid that Tom had escorted down the aisle as part of the bridal party processional.

"Terrific job, Brenna." Tom gave the woman a thumbs-up.

That was kind of him to say. Even though all a bridesmaid had to do was glide down the aisle and stand there without calling attention to herself, it wasn't as easy as it looked, especially, if like Jude, you had a touch of social anxiety. She'd done the bridesmaid two-step more times than she cared to count.

Thirteen to be exact.

She'd been a bridesmaid thirteen times. Not quite as bad as the heroine in *27 Dresses* but she was getting there.

The guest-book blonde cornered Tom as soon as

they walked into the reception room for the cocktail hour. "You look great in that tux, Tom."

"So did the fifty guys who wore it before me, Carla."

"I'll bet you can't wait to get out of it," she trilled.

"If I need any help, I'll let you know."

"I wish I could speak my mind like that," Jude mumbled after Carla moved on. "I'm just too shy."

"Carla's a bundle of energy. She put the 'f' in fun."

"*I* want to be a lot of fun."

"Then just relax," he soothed in his sexy-as-sin voice. "And have a good time."

"I'm working on it." She gulped.

"Practice makes perfect." He grinned and gently put his hand to her upper back to guide her through the crowd. "Can I get you a drink?"

She liked his hand on her. Was that smart? Honestly, all she knew about him was what she'd found on a quick internet search. Tom Brunswick had an active life, a social media presence, and a website for his furniture business that had garnered over a thousand five-star reviews. She was impressed.

"A ginger ale would be nice, thank you," she said, both disappointed and relieved that he'd have to retract his hand in order to fetch the drinks.

"How about white wine spritzer just to loosen up

a little? You did say you wanted to get rid of that Goody Two-Shoes image."

"Do I *have* to drink?"

"Nope, you don't have to do anything you don't want to do. That's the point. I'll get the ginger ale."

"Thank you."

"Be right back." He waved and took off.

Leaving Jude feeling like an island solitary in a sea of happy people.

4

ude watched as Tom joined a small crowd milling around the wet bar, then scanned the room, wishing she knew someone with whom to strike up a conversation.

A handsome man strolled up, curious interest in his dark eyes. "Did I just see you with Tom?"

"Yes, but we're just friends."

"Then Tom's dumber than I thought." The man raked an appreciative gaze over her body.

"Excuse me?"

"Hi, I'm Dirk." He stuck out a hand. "Tom's college roommate."

"Nice to meet you, Dirk." She shook his hand. "Do you have a last name?"

"I'm glad you asked that. Actually, I'm quite proud

of my family name, even though it's a little unusual. Poomph. Dirk Poomph. Rhymes with *oomph*."

The man was certainly forward. Not the type she normally went in for, but maybe that was a good thing. She was here to kick up her heels after all.

"Goodbye, Poomph," Tom said, coming to stand beside her with drinks in his hands.

"Just getting acquainted with your new friend, Thomas."

"Don't be a creeper, Dirk."

The two men stared at each other like front-runners in a footrace, their gazes locked in some kind of long-term testosterone clash.

Hmm, what was that about?

"Nice meeting you, Jude."

"You too."

"Save a dance for me." Smiling, Dirk shrugged good-naturedly and sauntered away, hands in his pockets to hike up his jacket and stretch the navy slacks tight across his butt.

"Was he pestering you?" Tom asked.

She shook her head and accepted the ginger ale in a champagne flute. "You don't need to play bodyguard. I'm here to have fun."

"I thought I was going to be the one you had fun with."

"Aww, are you jealous?" She canted her head and shot him a teasing grin.

"Of Dirk?" He snorted.

"You *are* jealous." She took a sip of her ginger ale, peering at him over the rim of the champagne flute.

"No way." He rolled his eyes.

"Don't worry, I'm not chasing after your college roommate. He just seemed like a good person to practice flirting with so that I can attract the man of my dreams."

"Wait, what? I thought you wanted to be wild and free and use a successful wedding to get over a failed one."

"That too. First. *Then* I want to find a keeper."

"Those are opposing goals. Pick one. Do you want to be wild and free or do you want to get married?"

"Why does it have to be either/or?"

"You *can* have both, just not at the same time." His smile sent a hot flare of heat up her spine. He should be penalized for hitting below the belt. The smile was unnerving. "Pick one."

"I do want to get married eventually. I'm old-fashioned that way."

He seemed disappointed in her and that dismayed Jude in a way she hadn't expected. She wanted Tom's approval.

"But for now," she amended quickly. I want to be

bold. Brave. Brazen. Wild and free. That's what I want...for now."

Relief shown in his eyes, but he shook his head. "Jude—"

"I know that look. You think I'm an impossible case. Next you'll tell me to be myself, and I can tell you how well that works."

Before he could respond, Tara and Ben made their grand entrance and the party began in earnest with the wedding planner rushing around shooing everyone to take their seats for the meal.

Tom guided her to their assigned seats just as servers passed through the crowd with the food. Filet mignon was on the menu. Since Jude had planned a wedding the previous year, she knew exactly how much that option cost. Tara and Ben were pulling out all the stops.

The food was delicious, and the toasts that followed were fun and lively. Tom's speech to his twin and her new husband was heartfelt and humorous and had the crowd alternating between uproarious laughter and dabbing at misty eyes.

He possessed an undeniable presence, and he was a master at holding the audience's attention. Jude was in danger of developing an insta-crush on the man. He was everything she was not—poised, energetic, and self-confident. An intoxicating cocktail of competent masculinity. From what she'd seen of him so far, he had a charming way of making people feel at ease, and he seemed to relish his role as entertainer.

No wonder she was drawn to him.

And she wasn't the only one. By nature, Jude was an observer, preferring the sidelines to the spotlight. While Tom worked up the guests with his stories, Jude people-watched and found herself fascinated.

She saw Tara and Ben share enchanted glances, noticed Tom's parents looking proud and putting their heads together in parental satisfaction, and spied the guest-book blonde giving Tom the side-eye. And later, after the speeches and before the dancing started, the lull when many people headed to the restrooms, she observed Dirk and Tara having a powwow behind the wedding party table. When they both simultaneously looked across the room at her, she felt a current of energy shoot through her body, and Jude knew without a shadow of a doubt that they were talking about her.

What were they saying?

Self-conscious, she made a beeline for the restroom as well. Upon exiting, she found Tom waiting for her.

"Hi," he greeted her with his rakish grin.

"Hey." She couldn't help smiling back.

"How you doing?" He seemed to genuinely want to know.

"Good. I'm having a good time."

"Wanna dance?"

"What?"

"Simple question. Do you want to dance?"

"We can't dance yet. The bride and groom aren't dancing," she said.

"Do you hear music?"

"Well, yes, they've just started playing, but the bride and groom always dance first—"

"A bold woman breaks with tradition. If you want to stop being so nice, stop caring so much what people think."

"But I can't ruin your sister's special day."

"Look at it as getting the party started. Besides, if it ticks her off—which it won't—Tara will blame me, not you."

"Um..."

Without giving her a chance to back out, he led her to the empty dance floor and caught her up in his arms.

"Wait," he said.

"Did you change your mind?" she asked. "Feels too weird?"

"Not at all. Give me your shoes."

"Huh?"

"Give me your shoes."

It seemed an odd request, but perhaps he feared she'd tromp on him with her stilettos. "I won't step on your toes. I promise. I'm a pretty good dancer."

"Glad to hear it. But I don't want you breaking your neck in those things." He bent and lifted one of her feet, removing her four-inch stiletto.

Aware of a few curious glances, she quickly slipped out of the other shoe, and he stuffed one in each of his jacket pockets.

"Now they'll all know you're here to party," he said wickedly.

His hand was low on her hip and his breath was warm on her forehead. They couldn't have been more in sync if she'd been standing on top of his feet. She turned her head to the side, afraid of smearing lipstick on his gleaming white shirt, but he bent and pressed his cheek against hers.

It was a tango position, but he managed to dance that way to the band's sentimental slow number, "Can't Help Falling in Love."

No one else joined them on the dance floor. All they needed was an overhead floodlight to qualify as the featured attraction.

That made her uncomfortable. This wasn't her night. This wasn't her wedding. Guilt did a number on her. She didn't know these people. She shouldn't be here. As a private person and an introvert, the sudden attention unnerved her, and Jude stopped dancing.

"What's wrong?" Tom asked, still trying to drag her around the dance floor.

"I can't do this."

"Do what?"

"This." Unnerved, Jude snatched her shoes from Tom's pockets, and holding them tightly in her hands, she raced from the room.

CONCERNED, TOM WENT AFTER HER. WAS SHE having flashbacks to her wedding day that ended so differently from Tara and Ben's? When he'd invited her as his date, he hadn't even thought about how attending a wedding might affect her psychologically.

How inconsiderate.

Contrite, he found her in the hallway.

Barefooted, she sidled up to the nearest wall for a place to steady herself while she put her shoes back on. She looked, he noticed, a bit panicky.

"Hey," he said, surprised to hear his voice come out low, husky, and gentle. "Are you okay?"

"Yes, sure, fine, why do you ask?" Avoiding his

gaze, she bent to slip her finger at the back of her shoe to help ease her foot into it.

"You sure?"

"Perfectly. Absolutely. One hundred percent."

"You ran off the dance floor like your hair was on fire," he said. "Why?"

"I told you I felt uncomfortable dancing before your sister and her husband. You put the focus on us. That's not right."

"Tara and Ben don't care. I promise."

"*I* care."

"Are you that married to tradition?"

"I'm a rule follower. You got me. That's why Jaxon dumped me. I'm too rigid."

That reasoning shocked him. "No, you're not."

"I'm uncomfortable upstaging the bride and groom."

"One, we didn't upstage them, and two, I've always believed we only grow when we're outside our comfort zones. You did ask me to give you some pointers as to what you're doing to turn off guys. Being too rigid is one of those things."

She got her shoes on and finally raised her head to meet his gaze. "Meaning?"

"If you want to be a bold woman, you're gonna have to get comfortable with being uncomfortable."

"I think I've made a big mistake trying to

change." She gave a forlorn shake of her head. "There's nothing wrong with being nice."

"Nothing at all." He stepped closer.

Tom had the feeling that Jude would have backed up if she'd had anywhere to go. "Other people are on the dance floor now."

He nodded toward the ballroom where, through the open door, he could see his twin and her new husband swaying to "Unchained Melody."

Jude bit down on her bottom lip.

Tom took another step closer. "Unless your fear is about more than an empty dance floor."

Her face flushed. From dancing? Or something else? She'd been drinking ginger ale so the flush wasn't from alcohol.

He held out his hand to her. "May I have this dance?"

Mutely, she nodded and accepted his hand.

Tom led her back to ballroom and the dance floor.

Her hand felt small in his, and when he slipped his hand around her waist, she melted against him, making him feel big, clumsy—and far too aroused.

He lowered his eyelids, but he was anything but sleepy. The sooner she hooked up with someone else, the better for his libido.

Whether she admitted it or not, she was looking

for a lot more than just a good time, although he couldn't even give her that. He had taken a forty-day vow of celibacy, and he was determined to win that bet.

Besides, no matter how hard she tried to change her personality, she was a *nice* woman, sexy black dress and stilettos be damned.

He drew her closer.

She didn't resist.

Why was he tempting fate? He wanted to win that bar bet more than anything, to prove he was the "master of his domain," to steal a quote from an old *Seinfeld* episode called "The Contest," but she was clouding his thinking, wrecking his self-control, and unwittingly leading him into temptation.

Her firm, lush breasts were crushed against his chest, and his jacket and her dress weren't armor enough to keep him from imagining her nipples against his bare skin.

Unexpectedly, she slid both hands around his neck and tugged his head down so she could whisper in his ear. "Thank you for tonight. I needed this more than I knew."

The light whisper of her breath against his ear sent shock waves to his groin, but then she let go of his neck and put distance between them again. She was achingly appealing in her sweetness. No matter how much she claimed to want to let loose and take a walk on the wild side, women like Jude came with strings attached, and he wasn't ready for that.

Honestly? He didn't know if he ever would be. No matter how happy his twin and her new husband looked in their married bliss, Tom wasn't looking for entanglement.

The song ended, and then the lights dimmed for a romantic waltz.

"May I cut in?"

Tom felt a tap on his shoulder and glanced over to see Dirk grinning at him. Narrowing his eyes, he wondered what his buddy was up to. He knew Dirk would do anything to win the bet. Was he trying to stoke Tom's jealousy and fuel his feelings for Jude? It wouldn't be the first time he pulled something underhanded.

"Buzz off, Poomph," Tom growled.

"Oh." Dirk pointed his fingers as if they were six-shooters at Tom. "I just heard. Jake's out. So it's just me and you, amigo."

Once again, the challenge came down to the two of them. They stared hard at each other. This wasn't the time or place to discuss the bet.

"I'd like to cut in," Dirk repeated.

Tom didn't want to let him.

Jude cleared her throat and inclined her head toward Dirk.

Tom lifted an eyebrow and felt a strange ache in the center of his chest. "Do you *want* to dance with him?"

She smiled softly and offered a half shrug. "How wild and free can I be if I only dance with one man the entire night?"

"Okay," Tom said, surprised by the disappointment sinking to the bottom of his shoes. What was that all about? He didn't care if she danced with other guys, just why did it have to be Dirk? "If that's what you want."

"It is," she said, but he could have sworn he spied uncertainty in her blue eyes.

"Looks like I win." Dirk smirked and muscled him aside.

Narrowing his eyes, Tom gritted his teeth and felt another tap on his shoulder as Jude accepted Dirk's arm and waltzed off.

"Hi! I see you're in need of a partner."

He turned to see Brenna Butler standing beside him. Brenna flew for the same small airline that Tara did. He'd heard a lot about Brenna from his sister, but they'd just met in person for the first time at last night's rehearsal dinner. Before the no-sex bar bet and before meeting Jude, Tom would have been lobbying for Brenna's phone number, but now things were just too complicated for a hookup with this vivacious woman.

"Dance with me." Brenna took his hand. Now here was a bold woman who knew what she wanted. Casual, free. The type he was usually attracted to.

Normally, he liked the no-strings-attached approach. So why was he missing Jude's girl-next-door style? His gaze trailed to the dance floor where Dirk's hand was resting too low on Jude's back for Tom's liking.

Frowning, he let Brenna lead him into the waltz.

"I'm really glad I finally got to meet Tara's sexy brother," Brenna cooed. "I had no idea you were so hot."

"Uh-huh," he said, not really paying attention. Honestly, if Dirk moved his hand one inch lower on Jude's backside, he was cutting in and putting a stop to this nonsense.

He's just trying to get under your skin. Don't take the bait.

Yes, but from what he could tell, Jude was rather naïve and just playing at being an adventuresome woman. She had no idea Dirk was a renowned heartbreaker, and if he set his sights on her, she was in over her head.

Jude didn't stop with Dirk.

As the hours ticked by, she danced with partner after partner, waving occasionally to Tom as she whirled past him where he'd ended up brooding in the corner nursing a beer. When she wasn't dancing, she was flitting around, introducing herself to the other guests and engaging in rapt conversations with his relatives.

She really did take an interest in people, Tom noticed, liking that about her.

The final dance was the Chicken Dance, and everyone had uproarious fun. Jude returned for him at last, dragging him onto the dance floor to waggle his body like a chicken to the polka.

Jude beamed, a sheen of perspiration dotting her forehead. She was having a blast. Tom tried to get into the spirit, but then Dirk came wiggling over to bump his hip against Jude's, and Tom had to bite his tongue to keep from saying something that would put him in an unfavorable light.

The dance ended and the reception was over.

Jude turned to thank Dirk for a lovely evening. Gritting his teeth, he waited while Dirk gave Jude a quick hug and then sent Tom a sly wink.

"Are you ready to go?" Tom asked her.

Jude turned to study him, hair tousled, face flushed, a feral gleam in her eyes.

Whoa. Tom gulped. She was taking this wild woman thing seriously.

"Dirk's offered to give me a ride home," she said.

"What?"

"I'm giving her a lift home," Dirk said as if it was settled.

Tom stepped closer to Jude. "I brought you here, and *I'm* making sure you get home safely."

Dirk smiled wolfishly, and Tom knew that's exactly what his buddy had been angling for. Get and keep Tom in close proximity with Jude, especially when she looked so hot and friendly. Dirk was anxious to win that bet.

Yeah, well, not happening. He would *not* have sex with Jude under any circumstances. Tom met his buddy's gaze, shook his head, and mouthed, *I'm winning the bet this time*.

"She came with me, Poomph; she's leaving with me." Tom jutted out his chin.

"Message received." Dirk's grin widened and he lifted a hand to wave goodbye to Jude and called over his shoulder on the way out the door, "Have fun, you two, but don't do anything I wouldn't do."

Tom grunted and took hold of Jude's elbow.

Jude's eyes flared even brighter, and he wondered how much champagne she'd downed over the course of the evening. So much for just ginger ale. "You *are* jealous of him."

He liked it when she was lippy. Meek, submissive women weren't for him—but neither was Jude Bailey. "Of a guy named Poomph? You gotta be kidding."

"If you're not jealous," she asked, "why are your earlobes turning red?"

Tom resisted the urge to cover his ears and snorted. "It's been a long night."

"Uh-huh." She laughed all the way to the coat check.

Haha. Funny stuff. He wasn't jealous of Dirk. But when they stepped outside to find the steps slick from where it had rained while they'd been inside dancing, Tom couldn't help thinking he sure as heck wasn't going to let his buddy win that bet.

He had one rule tonight. One rule only.

Hands off Jude.

Too bad she'd already slipped her arm through his and was looking up at him as if he were a juicy T-bone steak and she hadn't eaten in weeks.

꽃 5 꽃

Tom's car must have shrunk in the rain.

The restored '65 Mustang had seemed too small for Tom's broad shoulders and long legs on the way to the wedding, but now he filled it like an oyster in its shell.

Jude kept her arms pressed to her sides to avoid brushing against him and her knees locked together so she wouldn't knock against his fingers clutching the manual gear shifter. Taking his arm for him to help her down the steps in her stilettos had been a mistake. The minute she'd touched him, her body got all warm and tingly.

Even if they weren't actually touching now, he got inside her every time she inhaled, his aftershave sweeping through her head. Actually the scent made her a little dizzy. Or maybe that was the champagne Dirk had brought her.

Dirk had been a really good dancer, but who could think of him when Tom was sitting right beside her, upending her senses and scrambling her brain? And when he'd asked politely for her phone number, she'd given it to him.

Why not? She was on a journey of self-exploration.

"You really didn't have to take me home." She was repeating herself, but what else was there to say to a man this handsome?

"Just think of me as your designated Uber."

"I had two glasses of champagne."

"I noticed you'd switched from ginger ale."

"You were watching me?"

"Believe it or not, you're pretty watchable, Jude."

Darn it, why did she have to blush so easily? She turned to look out the window to hide her face from him. The streetlights had illuminous halos around them in the damp night air, and they drove the remainder of the way to her place in silence.

He parked his car at the curb in front of her complex. "I'll walk you to your door."

"No need." Jude unbuckled the seat belt and hopped out. She was quick, but Tom was quicker. He met her on her side of the car.

THE MAKESHIFT GROOM

With a dark coat flapping around the satin-striped trousers of his tux, he could pass as a template for an aristocratic playboy. Only his unruly hair didn't fit the slick image.

"Seriously, no need to walk me up." Her palms had grown sweaty, and she clasped them together.

"Indulge me. I aim to deliver you to your door safe and sound."

"Is that what you're doing?" She hadn't intended to giggle, but it slipped out.

"Is it so far-fetched that I might have manners?"

"No, of course not." Another giggle. Damn, maybe she had *had* too much champagne. She was a lightweight when it came to alcohol, which is why she rarely drank.

"Portal to portal." He gestured for her to proceed him up the first flight of stairs. "The gentleman's code."

They walked up the three flights of stairs to her landing.

"I had a good time. Thanks," she said in front of her door, attributing her slight breathiness to the third-floor climb in stilettos. "If you'll wait just a minute, I'll go get you the Bulls tickets. You held up your end of the bargain; it's time for me to uphold mine. I had a fabulous time tonight, thanks to you."

"I'M NOT TAKING YOUR TICKETS," TOM SAID WHEN Jude returned to the foyer where she'd left him while she dashed into the kitchen. "I didn't do anything to earn them."

"You gave me a nice night on the town, and I met a handsome man—"

"Aw, shucks," he said, ducking his head and feigning toeing the floor with his patent leather shoe like an embarrassed little boy.

"Oh," she said, laughing. "I meant Dirk, but you're handsome too. He gave me his phone number." She patted the clutch purse she still held in her hand.

Of course he did. Tom grunted. He was about to say, *I don't think Dirk is the guy for you*, but he didn't want to sound petty. He was *not* jealous of Dirk. Yes, in college, Dirk had stolen Tom's girlfriend and then unceremoniously dumped her, but they'd been living in the same frat house and eventually he'd forgiven his buddy. Dirk had claimed he'd hooked up with Amanda to show Tom that he couldn't trust her, and he'd been right.

But the thought of Dirk being with Jude had Tom gritting his teeth.

"You've already missed one of the games," Jude

was saying, extending the tickets toward him. "Please take them."

He'd feel like a jerk if he took her valuable season tickets for doing nothing more than escorting her to a wedding.

"At least let me pay for them."

"No, we had a deal. I had a great time, but in retrospect it was a silly idea—asking you to help me loosen up and shed my niceness. You can't do that kind of inner work for me."

"Hey, you went to the head of the class tonight," he murmured.

"Nah, I am who I am. I'm nice. I might as well accept that I'm never going to be a glamour-puss like the gorgeous bridesmaid you were dancing with."

"Brenna?" Tom shook his head. "She's attractive, don't get me wrong, but there's just no *zing* there, if you know what I mean."

"Really?" She appeared surprised. "I thought she oozed *zing*."

Her eyes widened and she looked so hopeful that Tom almost turned tail and ran. *Remember the bet!* If he stayed here, he was going to kiss her and that was a no-no.

Her cheeks were a glowing pink, either from the cold outside or the overheated air between them.

Lightly, she moistened her lips and he couldn't pry his gaze from her little tongue.

In that moment, he wanted to kiss her more than he wanted to breathe. Despite her hard-luck history with men, Jude was dangerous. Especially to him. At least for the next month. He had a bet to win.

After that? All bets were off, pun intended.

Dirk had certainly known what he was doing by hitting on Jude in front of Tom. He was feeling far more possessive of Jude than he had any right to feel. His emotions unnerved him.

She was too adorable and sexy in that dress and heels. A sweet kittenish look that could drive any guy bonkers.

"I better get going," he said.

"The tickets." She flapped them at him.

He held up a palm. "I can't."

"Please?"

He really did love the Bulls. He stared at the tickets she was thrusting in his direction, still reluctant to take them. "I—"

"Here," she said, slipping the envelope into his coat pocket in one smooth movement that put her far too close to him.

"I haven't done enough to earn them," he protested.

"*Yet*," she said and opened the door.

He raised an eyebrow, far more intrigued than he should be. "Yet?"

"Good night, Tom." She shooed him over the threshold.

He stepped outside, turned back to say good night....

That's when she went up on her tiptoes, leaned in, and kissed him on the cheek. Certainly not a sexy kiss, but it blew his socks right off. Good thing she was strictly off-limits. He dipped his head, his gaze fixed on her lips.

"Good night, Tom," she repeated in a firmer voice.

"Night," he said, feeling crazily relieved and madly disappointed at the same time. "And thanks a lot for the tickets."

"Jaxon will eat his heart out."

He didn't immediately remember who Jaxon was and by the time he recalled her ex-fiancé's name, he'd raced down three flights of steps and ran to his car in a downpour, wishing he could turn around, go back, and spend the night.

And that was why he zoomed out of her neighborhood as fast as the speed limit allowed.

TOM WOKE UP SLOWLY AND RELUCTANTLY THE NEXT morning, squinting against the bright winter sun streaming through half-closed blinds. His mouth was dry, and he felt headachy. He should have drank more water last night after the champagne and beer at the wedding.

The cell phone penetrated his skull on its fourth shrill ring, but he wasn't going to answer. He was supposed to be at his parents' house for brunch with Tara and Ben before they left for their honeymoon in Fiji, and he really didn't want to go.

"Ridiculous," he muttered sullenly.

Tara and Ben would be so wrapped up in each other they wouldn't even notice who else was in the room. He didn't see the point of going, but his sainted mother had slaved over the brunch, so he knew he had to drag his lazy carcass over there.

Grr.

The phone rang again.

Wincing, he pushed away the covers, shivering as he went into the kitchen, picking up the phone along the way.

Instead of answering, he let it go to voicemail while he brewed coffee and then ran through his text messages—there was a sultry "I loved dancing with you last night" from Brenna, an invitation to some friend's upcoming bachelor party—why was everyone suddenly getting married—and a gloaty question from Dirk, asking if Tom was still in the competition after his night with Jude.

"You better believe it," Tom muttered and immediately the image of Jude's face, after she'd kissed his cheek, popped into his head.

He wasn't one to kid himself. She was a looker, funny and sweet, too. He certainly wouldn't mind taking her to bed—after he won the bet, of course—but she deserved better than that. She was the kind of girl you brought home to meet mother, and that's just not where Tom's head was at.

Brunch was nice. Nicer than he expected. The food was delicious and the conversation lively. It was fun watching his twin with her new husband. They did look so rapturously in love that he couldn't help feeling a little envious, even though he was a long way from wanting the "I do" for himself.

When he hugged Tara goodbye before she and Ben left for the airport, his heart filled with happiness for his sister and he told her so.

"You'll get there, bro. You can't hurry love."

"Who says I want love?" he asked her.

"Everyone wants love," Ben said and leaned over to kiss Tara's cheek. "You're just slow to admit it."

She sank against him and sighed.

His sister and Ben did make marriage seem enticing,

and for some strange reason, he liked that radical thought. Jude was in his head again, and he saw her going up on those sexy high heels, her lush hair tumbling over her shoulders, her full pink lips puckered, kissing him...

One kiss, Brunswick. It was one kiss and a cheek kiss at that. Slow your damn roll.

Yes, yes. Great advice. Still, he had to admit, Jude rattled him. Who knew niceness was such a turn-on? And what in the hell was wrong with her ex-fiancé?

After brunch, he hit the gym, putting himself through a punishing high-intensity routine designed to push aside thoughts of Jude and the goofy bar bet that prevented him from just picking up the phone, calling her, and asking her out. That's what strenuous exercise was good for. Wearing a man out so he wouldn't think about a certain blue-eyed lady with gorgeous legs and a killer smile.

Once he was back at his apartment, he checked his text messages again.

One was from Brenna.

Hi, Tom. Remember me? UR probably surprised 2 hear from me again so soon, but my schedule got changed. I'm flying out of O'Hare for Costa Rica tomorrow. And guess what? I'm available 2night—all night. Love 2 see you.

Hmm. Should he ignore her text? Normally, he'd

jump up and clean the house in anticipation for an evening romp with her, but he really wanted to win that bet. Plus, there was Jude. For some illogical reason, he couldn't shake her from his head.

His cell phone buzzed in his hand. Not a text this time. Brenna was calling.

Not really sure why, he answered. "Hello?"

"So, Tommy, did you get my text?" Brenna purred with all the subtlety of his Mustang's eight-cylinder engine.

Tom grimaced. He hated being called Tommy. He'd left that nickname behind in the fifth grade. "Just saw it."

"You don't keep your phone with you at all times?" Brenna sounded astonished that his phone wasn't fused to his body.

"I was at the gym."

"Ahh," she said, and an even sexier tone curled into her voice. "I wish I'd known. I would have come by to work out with you. It's been such a long time since I've worked up a vigorous sweat, and all those hours in the *cock*pit take a toil."

The woman was attractive and an airline pilot, very impressive. Plus, she was ready and eager for a hookup. If it hadn't been for that no-sex bet...

Tell the truth. Not being interested in Brenna has as

much to do with your attraction to Jude as it does that dumb contest.

"Yeah, you see, that's just it..." Tom trailed off.

"What's just it?" Brenna sounded as bright as a new coin.

"This is bad timing."

"How so?"

"Um...I'm in the middle of a forty-day ice bucket challenge."

"Ice bucket challenge?" Brenna sounded confused and he didn't blame her. He was babbling. "I'm not following you."

Briefly, he explained about the celibacy challenge.

"You're actually serious?" She sounded incredulous and a little ticked off. "You'd pass up a night with me just because of a silly frat boy pact?"

All of sudden it occurred to him that Dirk might have put Brenna up to the phone call. It was so like his former roommate to keep throwing temptation at Tom.

"Nice try," he said.

"Huh?"

"Sexy as you are, Brenna, I'm not falling for it."

"Excuse me?" Her voice went up an octave on "me."

Okay, if Dirk was using her to foil Tom and get him to throw in the towel in order to be with Brenna, that meant she wasn't in on the fix, but that didn't mean Dirk hadn't manipulated her into calling. His friend was wily.

"By the way, where *did* you get my number? Was it Dirk Poomph?"

"What are you talking about?"

"Did Dirk put you up to calling me."

"No."

"You sure?"

"I did dance with Dirk last night, but he was completely complimentary about you." She was really starting to sound irritated now. "He said you were a great guy, if that's what you're getting at. But Tommy, I'm beginning to think otherwise. No, Dirk didn't give me your number. It was Tara."

"Oh." He paused. "Sorry to sound so suspicious, but Dirk is the one who instigated the bar bet, and I had to make sure you weren't in on trying to bring me down."

She was silent for a bit, then said in a tight voice, "I see."

"Yeah."

"You thought he was using me as a bait to lead you astray?"

"Sadly, I'm afraid so."

"He's not."

"I believe you."

"And yet, you'd still rather win this silly bet than spend the day with me?"

"I didn't say that. I can be with you in thirty-five days, after I win the bet. I'll be flush with cash and we can hit the swankiest restaurant in town."

Tom heard the sound of the connection being severed.

Brenna had hung up on him.

Well, darn. He was sorry she'd gotten caught up in Dirk's ploy, and he supposed he owed her an apology.

He texted her a remorseful emoji.

She texted back. Call me when you grow up.

Okay. He deserved that. He'd allowed Dirk to get inside his head. *Bring it on, Poomph. I can resist any woman you throw at me.*

But even as he thought it, Tom couldn't help feeling that Brenna made a good point. Why was he letting a decade long college rivalry control his love life?

Then she texted. FYI, Dirk did talk about your date last nite. A lot!!! I think he has a crush on Jude.

❧ 6 ❧

While Tom was brunching, hitting the gym, and disappointing Brenna, Jude slept in on Sunday morning after a night of dancing. The slow steady rain drumming on the roof made staying in bed easy.

Lazing, she drifted in and out of dreams about Tom Brunswick. Sexy dreams she had no business dreaming. She barely knew the guy, but wow, the dreams were *fun*.

Shortly before noon, her cell phone rang, yanking her from juicy visions of Tom showering beneath a Hawaiian waterfall. She grabbed for her phone, welcoming any call to jolt her back to reality.

The caller ID said "Unknown caller," but she answered it anyway.

"Jude Bailey?" asked a vaguely familiar male voice.

"Yes," she admitted guardedly, thinking of the quickest but kindest way to get rid of telemarketers.

"This is Dirk."

"Dirk?" She drew a blank.

"Dirk Poomph, rhymes with oomph. We danced at the wedding."

"Oh, sure. Hi, Dirk."

"How ya doing?"

Um, what was this about? "Great, just great."

"I thought maybe I'd put a little oomph in your life," he chuckled. "Say Saturday night? Ballroom dancing at my country club?"

"Are you asking me out?"

"That sounded kind of arrogant, didn't it?"

"A tad."

"Apologies. I just enjoyed dancing with you so much that I'm eager to do it again. What do you say?"

"Hmm..." She drew in a deep breath, still feeling a little hazy from those steamy dreams about Tom. "I appreciate the invitation, but I'm not really dating right now."

"No?"

"I got stood up at the altar six months ago, and I'm giving myself a year to hit the pause button on serious relationships. I'm not interested in a rebound man."

"What about Brunswick?"

"What about him?"

"You two aren't..." he trailed off.

"No, no, we're *not*."

"Oh," he said, sounding somewhat pensive. "Okay, I had to ask. If you change your mind about dancing, text me. Afterward, we could hit this great new restaurant I know about that stays open late."

And then just like that he hung up and Jude couldn't help feeling the guy had been on a fishing expedition, although she had no idea why she felt that way. Before she had time to ponder Dirk's motives, her mother phoned to fret about a family friend who was divorcing after thirty-seven years of marriage.

"I just can't understand it," Mom said for the twentieth time. "Why now after so many years together are Paul and Celeste calling it quits?"

"Mom, what I know about true love could get lost in a flea's pocket."

Her mother chuckled. "Dear, I don't think fleas have pockets, but I do love the way you've bounced back since Jaxon. Better for him to leave you at the altar than after decades of marriage like Celeste."

"I'm sorry to hear about Paul and Celeste. I can tell their breakup has upset you, but don't worry about Daddy. He'd not going to leave you."

"Of course he's not." Mom's voice took on a dreamy quality. "Your father and I are not just soul mates, we're best friends."

They were too. Whenever she saw her folks together, Jude couldn't help feeling she was missing out big-time. She'd been so desperate to find her soul mate she'd latched on to Jaxon and convinced herself that he was The One.

She was wiser now and wouldn't so easily jump into romantic relationships in the future. She'd made herself too available with Jaxon, always ready to drop whatever she was doing to make time for him. Well, no more of that nonsense. She wasn't twisting herself into a pretzel for some guy, not ever again.

Being on twenty-four-hour call whenever Jaxon wanted to see her had probably been a major blunder, much as it hurt to admit it now. Whenever she did finally marry, she wanted a union just like her parents, not Paul and Celeste.

Jude steered the conversation away from the divorcing couple, chatting with her mother about less stressful things than the end of a long-term marriage, while she padded into the kitchen to make coffee and avocado toast.

Finishing her call with her mother, she ate her very late breakfast, then cleaned up her dishes. After that, she Face-timed her cousin Leigh and told her all about the evening.

"So," Leigh said. "This Tom guy, he's a good dancer."

"Yes."

"And he's hot."

"Most definitely."

"Could there be romance in the air?"

"I'm not ready for that."

"Why not?"

"I want to find *me* before I get involved with anyone again. Besides, I'm not sure we'd be very compatible."

"Do you want me to tell you the story of how Max and I met again?" Leigh asked, referring to her husband, who was a crown prince. Literally.

"No, I remember."

"Just saying you might be more compatible than you originally thought."

"I'm not even entertaining thoughts like that."

"Don't close yourself off to possibilities."

"Thanks for the advice."

"Do you want a tour of the house?" Leigh asked.

"Thought you'd never ask."

For the next thirty minutes, Leigh carried her computer through her mansion, showing Jude her lavish home.

"I still can't believe you married a prince," Jude said.

"Hey, you never know what's around the next corner. Don't give up hope." Leigh gave her a pep talk, and then they said goodbye.

For the next four hours, Jude did laundry, read a book, watched the TV program *Natural Curiosities*, and marveled over the competitiveness of animals. It was a nice, relaxing Sunday afternoon. She wasn't expecting company so the door buzzer startled her, making her wonder whether to ignore it or answer.

Curiosity won out. She went to the intercom. "Who is it?"

"Tom Brunswick. May I come up?"

Her pulse quickened and her mind flew back to those sexy dreams. "Why?"

"Why not?"

"I'm still in my pajamas."

"I don't mind."

I just bet you don't.

"Please?" he said. "I'll wait down here while you get dressed."

"What do you want?" That sounded tacky and not the least bit like her, but her knees were already quivering at the thought of seeing him again. Especially since she'd kissed him last night like a total dumbbell.

On the cheek. It wasn't even a real kiss. No, but

her mouth had tingled for an hour afterward. Jude fingered her lips.

"I'd like to have a face-to-face conversation." He paused. "Please."

She hesitated, part of her wanting to tell him she was busy, even as another, hungrier part of her said, "Give me ten minutes and I'll buzz you up."

"SERIOUSLY, WHAT ON EARTH ARE YOU DOING here?" Jude asked from the open door of her apartment.

Panting after he'd sprinted up the three flights of stairs—*why* had he sprinted up three staircases—Tom couldn't answer right away. He pressed a hand to his chest and inhaled sharply.

Her big blue eyes widened. "Are you all right?"

He gasped, then nodded. Was his face as flushed as he feared?

"Um, do you need a glass of water?"

He waved away her question. "I...er...I happened to be in the area, and you popped into my mind and I thought, 'hey, why not see if Jude is home.'"

"All right, I'll buy that." Her nose crinkled and her eyes narrowed. "But *why*?"

Yeah, Brunswick, why?

She chuffed out a big breath of air as if she'd been the one to run three flights of stairs. Yes, he was yammering on about the stairs, but he'd been running really fast and it wiped him out, especially after ninety minutes in the gym that morning.

"C'mon in then." She motioned him over the threshold.

Yay! Why did he feel like he'd won a hundred dollars on a lottery scratch-off?

He slipped inside her apartment, passing her as she stood beside the open door. Her scent—a comforting blend of old books, dried rose petals, and vanilla bean—teased his nose as he sauntered past.

"Have a seat." She gestured at the couch.

He sat down as he watched her take the plump armchair across from him. He couldn't help smiling at her. She had that effect on him.

Niceness beget niceness.

She pressed her knees together a little primly and settled her joined hands into her lap.

"Now, tell the truth. Why did you drop in on me?"

"You *did* ask me to help you shake off the niceness."

"Turns out it was a rhetorical question."

He raised an eyebrow, studying her intently. "Backtracking?"

"What?"

"Rhetorical is not the way I remember it. In fact, you said, and I quote, 'Just give me some advice on how I can be a little bolder, a little less 'nice,' and the tickets are yours.'"

She crinkled her nose in that adorable way of hers. Like a bunny rabbit suspicious in new surroundings. "I did? That's terribly specific."

"It's why I'm here." He latched on to the excuse because it was all he had. He couldn't very well come right out and admit he simply couldn't get her out of his mind.

But coming here was pretty stupid if he really intended on winning that no-sex bet with Dirk. Just seeing her flawless skin and the way the fluffy blue sweater she wore hugged her curves had him thinking sexy thoughts he shouldn't entertain.

"You're here to earn your tickets?" She leveled him a skeptical stare.

"Yes."

"You could have called or texted first."

He nodded. "I should have. Spur of the moment impulses have gotten me into trouble more than once."

Which was how he'd lost the bar bet the first time around.

"I can imagine," she said dryly as if she disapproved of impulsiveness, but her eyes were smiling.

He had a sneaky suspicion she was baiting him, and he suspected she had a wicked sense of humor when you got to know her, but she'd met her match if she thought he was easily chased off. Tom loved a challenge. Hence the fix he was in.

She crossed her legs and swung her foot in lazy circles. She wore leggings in a wild, colorful pattern, and he couldn't stop staring at them. "Your friend Dirk called me."

"Wait, what?" Tom straightened his spine, surprised at how quickly his throat constricted. That rascal Dirk was up to no good.

"He asked me out."

"Yeah?" Tom raised an eyebrow, trying to look mild and chill, but inside he was steamed that Dirk was making a real play for Jude.

He knew what his buddy was up to, trying to stir Tom's jealousy. If Tom got protective over Jude that would only fuel the sexy feelings raging inside him, and such feelings could easily lead to the bedroom, especially since Jude was aiming for wild, loose, and bold.

But Tom refused to get possessive...at least outwardly.

"Yes." Jude was watching him as intently as a cat watching a mouse hole.

"You're going out with him?"

"No."

Whew! Tom was so relieved that he ran the back of his hand over his forehead. "What did he say when you turned him down?"

"He told me to text him if I changed my mind."

Tom paused, alarmed to find his body tensing in all kinds of places. "Why *did* you turn him down? Especially when you're aching to explore your wilder side? Why not say yes?"

Her smile turned coy and she lowered her gaze. "Because there's someone else I'm interested in."

"Oh?" he said, a torque of fresh jealousy twisting him up inside. She'd danced with a lot of guys last night and he mentally ran through them all. What was this all about? He barely knew Jude. She did, however, smell quite lovely and what a smoking hot body!

"And I was wondering..." Her shapely leg kept swaying.

Tom stared, mesmerized. "Yes?"

"The guy—"

"Is it Dirk?"

"No, forget Dirk. The guy who caught my interest doesn't go for women like me."

"What does that mean, Jude?"

Her cheeks pinked and she lowered her gaze. "I'm too dull for him."

"How do you know?"

"I talked to some of his relatives last night." Her gaze popped back up to his face. "They told me he dates glamorous women with exciting careers..." She paused. "Like Brenna."

He didn't really want to help her snag this guy. He wanted to *be* the guy she snagged, but there was the whole competition with Dirk thing, and when he'd told Brenna about the bar bet, that had gone over like a concrete balloon. He kept thinking about Brenna's reaction, and it prevented him from coming clean with Jude about the wager.

He should just be honest and say, *Hey, I like you, but I can't get into a relationship for thirty-five more days;, could you hold off transforming yourself until then?*

But he couldn't take the risk that, like Brenna, Jude would find the idea of a no-sex bet between fraternity brothers childish and immature. It *was* childish. He knew that, but he wanted to win anyway. Dirk had bested him once too often. This time, Tom was determined to emerge the victor.

That didn't mean he couldn't help Jude in her quest for a hot fling. He could steer her clear of the wrong guys and maybe, when the bet was over, he could convince her that she should be dating him instead.

He rubbed his palms against his jean-clad thighs,

surprised to find he was feeling a little nervous. "Sure," he said. "I'll do what I can. I owe you for those tickets."

She grinned, and he was glad he'd come—impulsive or not. Spending time with Jude was a great way to pass a Sunday afternoon.

"So where do we start?"

"Tell me about this guy," he invited, leaning forward on the couch to rest his elbows on his thighs, interlacing his fingers and resting his chin on top of his joining hands. Although he really didn't want to know about the man she wanted, but at least it wasn't Dirk.

Her gaze locked on to his. "Well, he's very good-looking and a great dancer."

"You've danced with him?" Tom couldn't look away if a fire had spontaneously broken out in the room. "Was he at the wedding?"

Slowly, she nodded, her grin widening.

"Oh, okay," he said, trying to sound completely unconcerned, but his mind was spinning over the guest list, trying to figure out who she had her eye on. She'd danced with several guys. He hadn't been keeping track for sure. He'd spent time dancing too.

"What else do you know about him, other than he likes interesting women?"

"He's really sweet, although I don't think he

knows it. I think he has a playboy image from his college days that he hasn't yet shaken. But that's just a guess. I have no actual facts upon which to base that impression."

"What are some of his interests and hobbies? Do you know?"

Jude shrugged. "I dunno. That's the point of getting to know him. But first, I have to attract him. Let's start there."

"How do you know he's not already attracted to you?"

"Hello." She waved a hand. "Weren't you paying attention? I'm too nice for him."

"I'm not sure what you even mean by this nice thing. Do you mean you feel you're too sedate?"

"Yes. That." She pointed a finger at him. "Boring."

"So, it's just a matter of changing the way you dress?" He raked a gaze over her comfy clothes. He had no complaints about the leggings and a fluffy tunic sweater, but if she wanted to knock a guy's socks off, maybe she should try something more revealing.

"That and my interests. There's nothing more I enjoy than curling up with a good book or watching Netflix and calling for takeout. I know, I've been lectured on that before. Dullsville."

"From your ex-fiancé?"

"Among others." She sighed.

"So how do you normally find your dates?"

"Excuse me?" She looked a bit confused.

"Dating apps? Social groups? Church? Work?"

"Not dating apps. I tried it once." She shook her head. "The people I met all seemed like they were waiting for something better to show up. The Swipe Right culture."

"How did you meet your ex-fiancé?"

"At work. He coaches high school basketball."

"That must be tough. Having to see him every day after he dumped you."

"He doesn't work there anymore."

"That's good for your healing, I suppose."

"Definitely."

"So what do you see as the essential problem with your dating life?" Tom steepled his fingers and felt professorial. Was he giving off a Henry Higgins vibe? Is that why she was asking him to help her date other men?

"I don't want anything serious right now, but I've never been one for casual relationships. I believe you can tell from the first date if someone is boyfriend material or not."

Am I boyfriend material? he wondered.

Tom eyed her, taking in those soft cheeks, rounded chin, and perky smile. He got that she was built for commitment. "Attracting men isn't your problem—picking the best one is."

Her smiled slipped away and a frown took its place, creasing her forehead. "If you say one word about my mistake with Jaxon—"

"He's ancient history." He held out his hands in a gesture of surrender and was relieved when she stopped scowling. "But you're still holding on to the memory of what he did to you like it's a security blanket."

"I am?"

"That's how it looks from where I'm sitting."

She gave that some thought, stroking her chin with a thumb and forefinger. "What are you saying?"

"You're letting a man who walked away from you judge how you should be in the world. You're giving him too much control. And you're doing the same with other people's opinions too. For instance, this new guy you're attracted to who you believe thinks you are too nice. Don't change yourself for him. Be you. If he doesn't like you, his loss. Not everyone is going to like you and that's okay."

A sadness came into her eyes. "But I want everyone to like me."

"And that, dear woman, is where you're tripping yourself up. Your problem isn't that you're not wild enough."

"It's not?"

"No."

"What is my problem?"

"You care too much about what other people think."

She looked as if he's just thrown a dart at a huge target and hit it dead center of the bullseye. "You might be right."

"That's not niceness. That's being a doormat."

"Hey!"

"The truth hurts just as it sets you free. You sure you're ready to go down this road?"

She nodded. Vigorously. "Okay, let's start fresh. Can you teach me how to stop caring about what other people think?"

"I could put you on the right path, but only you can walk it."

"Okay." She bobbed her head. "Let's do this thing."

"Grab your coat."

"Now?"

"You have something better to do?"

"No."

He stood up, felt his pulse quicken. Darn but he loved a challenge.

"Where are we going?" she asked.

"Why?"

"I'd like to know how to dress for the occasion."

"You look fine just as you are."

"No way, these are my lying around on the couch clothes."

"Are you worried people will whisper behind your back about the woman who wears comfy clothes in public?" He snorted.

"No." Her chin jutted up defiantly, but her tone said she was lying. "It's for me, not them."

"Okay, if it makes you feel any better, put on a pair of jeans and some lipstick, and let's hit the road."

7

Knowing Tom was far righter than she wanted him to be, Jude slipped into her bedroom and locked the door behind her. There was one area where he was wrong though; he hadn't realized she was trying to tell him that *he* was the man she was interested in.

That's because she wasn't his type.

Last night at the wedding, she'd talked to Tom's aunts and mother. They'd all shaken their heads over the fact that Tom couldn't seem to settle down.

"He likes the girls who keep it light," Tom's mom had shaken her head. "The fast ones."

"Women," one of the aunts had corrected. "When they're over eighteen, these days, they like to be called women."

"That's because they *are* girls," another aunt

chimed in. "Just wait until someone calls them ma'am."

"No offense," Tom's mother apologized to Jude.

"None taken," she'd answered, but she'd thought, *Tom likes fast women. Be faster.*

Jude shimmied out of her leggings in the time it took to haul in a deep breath. She was going for the fastest clothes change world record, fearful he'd come to his senses and decide to just take off.

She dove into a pair of black slacks that she wore to work and exchanged the old sweater for a button-down blouse, her heart beating just a little too fast for her own good. She felt...well, excited.

Chillax, Bailey.

The important thing to remember was that this wasn't a date and primping of any kind was strictly uncalled for. She took down her ponytail and ran a brush through her wavy hair. Staring at herself in the mirror, she realized that looked far too sexy and pulled her hair back into the ponytail.

Much safer.

No self-respecting nice woman would dream of accepting a date from a drop-in. But a fast woman would. She liked the idea of being fast. It was less intimidating than the word "wild." Wild had connotations of reckless that scared her. Fast just meant being quick on the draw.

Stop rationalizing a last-minute date. He's waiting.

She allowed herself a quick dab of lipstick. Quick was casual; quick was imperative. No overdoing it. No dressing to impress.

Even if she wanted to impress him.

Jude met the eyes of her reflection. He hadn't picked up on the fact that he was the one she was interested. Not Dirk. Not any of the other guys she'd danced with at the wedding. Tom was who she wanted. What did she have to do to get him to see that?

Just tell him.

No. She couldn't come right out and tell him she wanted a casual hookup. It wasn't her M.O. But maybe by hanging out together he'd figure it out on his own.

That was her game plan anyway.

And if it fell apart, then she would have learned something valuable in the process. Honestly, a total win-win.

"Have fun," she told her reflection, then drew in her breath and added, "and dare to be just a little bit wilder."

HOLY MACKEREL.

Did Jude have any idea that the male imagination kicked into overdrive as soon as a woman put a closed door between her and the man aching to remove her clothing?

It was impossible not to think about her undressing just a few feet away with only that thin wooden barrier between them.

Heat flushed his body as Tom envisioned what she looked in her panties and bra. Did she wear chaste white cotton or something far sexier? Considering her personality, his money was on the former. Didn't matter. It was hot either way.

He groaned.

"Are you all right?" she asked from the other side of the door.

Crap! He hadn't realized he'd actually groaned out loud.

"Just banged my shin on the table," he lied, quickly sitting back down and crossing his legs to conceal any contrary evidence. He didn't want to scare her.

"Perv," he muttered, but she was so darn hot, and he was in this stupid bet which seemed to stir obsessive thoughts of sex. He must have been crazy to think he should come by and check on Jude.

Idiot, he silently chided himself.

He should just get up walk out the door, but he

didn't want to. The idea of spending the evening with Jude intrigued him no end.

And he'd promised to help her find herself in exchange for the Bulls tickets and stop trying to be someone she wasn't.

Because that was the real issue here.

Jude's niceness sprang from her desire to please others, but in order to finally please herself, she was going to have to let go of that 'good girl' conditioning and learn what *she* truly wanted from life.

Jude strolled from the bedroom wearing black slacks, a white button-down blouse, and simple gold jewelry. A librarian outfit if ever he'd seen one. She looked understated and brainy, not wild and bold. But he loved it.

She put on a waist-length white ski jacket, and they were on their way. His shop was in Roseville, so he knew this suburb pretty well even though he lived a ways off in South Barrett.

"You hungry?" he asked.

"Starved."

"What would you like to eat?"

"I don't care. I can eat anything. What are you in the mood for?"

You, he thought, but he didn't dare say it.

From Jude's gung ho stance on changing her image, it might be really easy to charm her into his bed, but he wouldn't do that. One, he had a bet to win, and two, even though Jude claimed to crave wildness, she really wanted someone to love and admire her for who she was, and he refused to take advantage of her vulnerability.

"Do you really want to stop caring what people think?" he asked.

"Yes!" Her enthusiastic reply let him know his task might not be as tough as he first thought.

"Then stop deferring to other people. Say what you want to eat."

"I don't want to control anyone else's choices."

"This isn't about control. You can always compromise. This is about having a preference and stating it. To tell you the truth, guys find it frustrating when the woman won't ever say what she likes. It's an annoying guessing game."

"Hmm."

Tom cast a glance over at Jude. She looked pensive, slowly tapping her chin with an index finger.

"You're saying that while I believe I'm being nice by letting my date choose the restaurant, I'm actually being annoying."

"Yes. That's it."

"Wow. I never considered it that way. Jaxon, my ex, never seemed to mind. He just picked a place and told me where we were going."

"Good thing Jaxon went bye-bye." He wasn't trying to be funny, but Jude broke out in gales of laughter so sweet he wanted to keep up her good spirits.

"I want pizza," she said.

"Pizza it is."

"Don't you want to negotiate?"

"Not this time. This time you get what you want. I know the perfect place to grab a slice and it's only five minutes from here."

"Rocky's?" she asked.

"You know that joint?"

"It's my favorite pizza restaurant in the city."

"Mine too!"

They grinned at each other, and he rounded the corner to the road that led to Rocky's Pizza Palace.

The restaurant was pleasingly gaudy with a ceiling of colored Christmas lights that stayed there permanently and pseudo-Roman columns that divided the sections of booths and tables. At this early hour they snagged a choice booth in the rear, far away from a group of rowdy teenagers trying to impress their dates, and a big family with spirited kids.

"What do you normally get when you come here?" he asked as they sat down and a server handed them menus.

"I don't need a menu," Jude said to the teenaged

server. To Tom, she said, "I love the Roman—Italian sausage, black olives, and artichoke hearts."

"No kidding? Me too." His laugh sounded a little too giddy and that gave Tom pause.

He really liked Jude, especially when she looked at him like he was the prize that she'd been coveting in a claw machine, but this level of nervousness was unexpected.

"I also like extra cheese." She grinned as if she'd just said something naughty.

"A large Roman," Tom said, passing his menu to the server as well. "Extra cheese."

"Provolone, parmesan, or mozzarella?" the server asked.

Tom and Jude's eyes met again and in unison they said, "Mozzarella."

"I like how gooey the mozzarella melts." Jude giggled.

"Nice and stringy." Tom joined in her laughter. They were just grabbing a pizza together, no big deal, but damn, he was having fun. Jude's beguiling enthusiasm did weird things to him and he didn't know where to file that information.

Slow down, buddy. Can't go there. Not yet. Not for over a month.

Why did he have to meet Jude while he was in the middle of that celibacy challenge with his buds?

"And to drink?" asked the server.

"Draft root beer in a frosted mug," Tom said.

"The same." Jude nodded.

Goose bumps broke out on Tom's arms and he had no explanation for it. Jude had

a way of looking directly into his eyes that unraveled him in a really nice way. She didn't use common feminine flirting body language, like wrinkling her nose, twirling her hair, running her finger from her chin down her throat, using the gestures to call attention to her pretty face.

He resolved to talk to her like a buddy—put a damper on the flames she stirred in him—but he was the one fidgeting.

"So," Tom said because he couldn't think of anything else to say. "Tell me about yourself."

"You know I'm a high school librarian."

"And you know I craft and sell artisan furniture."

"No," she said, sounding impressed. "I thought you sold furniture. I didn't know you were a carpenter too."

"That's how I started. But I couldn't make enough furniture on my own to keep up with the demand, so I started selling other artisans in my shop."

"I didn't know quality furniture was so lucrative."

"There's been a backlash to cheap, disposal furniture. These days, people are looking for things that last and are better for the environment."

"Lucky you! So nice you get to do work you love."

"Hey," he said. "I see what you did there."

"Did what?" She blinked, apparently clueless.

"I asked you to tell me about yourself, and you turned things back on me, rather than telling me about yourself in return."

"I did?"

"You did."

She lifted her shoulders to her ears and let them drop hard. "I don't like talking about myself much. I prefer to focus on the person I'm with."

"While that's great for connecting with people, it doesn't do much for finding out who *you* really are."

She dropped her gaze. "I guess that's the problem. I'm more interested in other people than I am myself."

"It's not a bad thing, but you lose yourself in that dynamic."

The look that came into her eyes told him she already knew that about herself.

"Why do you suppose that is?" he asked. "Why is someone else's opinion more important than your own?"

"I don't like to rock the boat?" She ended the sentence with a question mark in her voice. "Maybe?"

"And letting people know who you are is rocking the boat?"

"I dunno." She shrugged again but she still didn't meet his eyes. "People enjoy it when I encourage them to talk about themselves."

"People like your ex."

"Yes," she admitted. "I let Jaxon call all the shots —just the way my father does. Dad is ex-Army, retired major. It shows on him, and I guess, now that you've pointed it out, on me too."

"What does your dad do now?"

"He's in insurance. He's the guy who wants to make sure everyone is safe and protected."

"And your mom?"

"Believe it or not, my mother has never had a full-time job. She does play poker in a local tournament and she wins more than she loses, so that's a plus. How about your parents?"

The server slipped in with two frosted mugs of root beer and then scooted off.

"Don't think I didn't notice how you shifted the focus back on me again," Tom said. "But to answer your question, Dad's an airline mechanic. Mom helps out at my shop, but she used to run a day care center. She came from a big family and wanted six kids of her own, but after Tara and me, she couldn't have more. Now she's ballistic about grandkids." Chuckling, Tom rolled his eyes. "I'm hoping Tara will get on the stick and take the pressure off me."

"My brother Dean has two kids, but when it comes to grandchildren, I don't think grandmothers are ever satisfied. The more the better seems part of the granny manifesto."

"Why should they be satisfied? They get to play with kids, hype 'em up on sugar and fun, and then send them home to their parents."

"That's a little cynical." She laughed as if she didn't mind.

"Maybe." He grinned, ready to change the subject off children. "What's your favorite thing to do in your spare time?"

"Read."

"Granted." He bobbed his head. "But that feels job related. How do you relax and have fun?"

"Books."

He cleared his throat and spread his hands out on the tabletop. "Beyond books. Surely there are other activities that you enjoy."

"You mean like sex?" Her eyes didn't look so guile-less now.

Tom almost choked on the mouthful of root beer he'd just swallowed. "I-er...meant like ping-pong or badminton or mini-golf, but if sex is on the table..."

Holy salmon mousse, had he seriously just said that?

She touched the tip of her tongue to her upper lip and gave him a look so blisteringly sultry it was all he could do not to hustle her out of the restaurant and back to her place ASAP.

But twelve hundred dollars, knocking Dirk off this throne, and bragging rights were at stake. He wouldn't seduce Jude, no matter the green-light signals she kept shooting his way.

What if she actively tries to seduce you?

He studied her. Nah, she wasn't the type. But she was trying to push herself outside her comfort zone. It could happen. What then? Well, he'd cover that ground if they got to it.

The pizza came hot from the oven and when Tom served them each a piece on the plates provided, it trailed gooey cheese across the plates.

Jude unrolled her silverware bundle and took out a fork.

"You're going to eat pizza with a fork?"

"Just the first few bites—until it cools off and the cheese stops dripping." She shot him a glance and with a jolt, Tom realized by teasing her about her preferences, he was solidifying her erroneous belief that what she wanted didn't really matter.

He backpedaled. "I apologize for making fun. Eat your pizza however you like it."

"Thank you, Tom. I appreciate that." She canted

her head and widened her smile and cut off a bite of pizza with her fork and knife.

"Not that you need my permission."

"I don't, do I?" Her tongue caught a string of pale mozzarella and she sort of twirled it into her mouth.

He watched, fascinated, and forgot for a minute about his own food.

"It's sizzling," she gasped, "but delicious."

A bit of sauce was clinging to her upper lip where it formed a little bow. Without thinking, he reached across the table and blotted it on her napkin.

"Oh, wow, you must think I'm a sloppy eater." Her face flushed. "Is there some rule I'm breaking here?"

"None whatsoever."

He had no intention of telling her how sexy it was to watch her eat. He wasn't going to say anything to make her self-conscious about it. Jaxon, the dud ex-fiancé, must be an egomaniac to treat her the way he had. Then again, Jude had put up with his bad behavior.

Maybe that was how he could best help her. Teach her to set strong boundaries...

...and keep them.

❧ 8 ❧

Jude couldn't believe she'd eaten half of a large pizza. Tom kept encouraging her, and she went hog wild, enjoying his warm smile and witty ways. But now, her waistband was tight, and she kept yawning. Cheese made her sleepy and she'd ordered extra mozzarella.

Why?

Subconsciously, had she done it to put an early end to their evening? Or was she overthinking things?

The cold air outside revived her, but not enough to come up with a clever ploy for talking him out of escorting her upstairs. Not that she tried very hard. Even if this wasn't a real date, she'd enjoyed herself immensely.

In fact, as he killed the engine in the parking lot

of her complex, she blurted, "Would you like to come up for ice cream?"

"I better not." He patted his belly.

"Are you sure?" she asked, feeling both rebuffed and relieved. "It's Ben and Jerry's Chunky Monkey."

"The chunky part is what blows dessert for me."

Jude eyed him. "I don't know why you're worried. You don't have an ounce of fat on your body."

"Exactly. I stay away from the Chunky Monkey."

"How about coffee?" She should offer him a night-cap, but the closest thing she had to alcohol in her apartment was cooking sherry.

"Can't. I gotta work tomorrow."

"Me too," she admitted with a soft sigh.

He opened the car door and ran around to the passenger side as she was getting out. He had such good manners. Although car-door opening was not something she required in a date, it was pretty nice.

"I'll walk you to your door."

"No need," she said, sweeping aside her hurt feelings that he wasn't coming up.

"When would you like to get together again?" he asked as they went up the sidewalk.

"Get together again?" She blinked. "Oh, you mean for my anti-doormat lessons?"

Tom laughed until he couldn't catch his breath. After he'd finally composed himself, he said, "Dang it,

Jude, you have a terrific sense of humor. I admire the hell out of you."

She admired his admiration and that felt weird so she stared down at the cracks in the concrete. "How does Saturday night sound?"

"Good. Great. Perfect." He gave her a thumbs-up.

"Where should we go?" she asked. "What should we do?"

"We'll do whatever you want to do."

"I don't care—"

"Uh-uh." Tom raised a finger and waggled it at her. "No, no. From now on, whenever you have an opinion, want, wish, or desire, speak your mind."

"I can try."

"Just answer this question. What would *you* like to do?"

"Umm." She crinkled her nose. "I don't know."

"Well," he said. "Think about it because that's what we're doing."

"Listen." She hauled in a breath. "You do not have to walk up three flights of stairs. We can say goodbye right here in the parking lot."

"It's almost ten."

"I'll be fine. I go in and out of my apartment at night all the time. This is a quiet neighborhood. I feel completely safe."

"Are you sure?"

"Yes."

He hesitated. "If that's what you want."

"It is."

"Okay, then." His eyes met hers, but she couldn't tell what he was thinking.

"Well, I guess this is good night." Jude gulped and stood there, waiting and hoping and wishing he'd give her a goodnight kiss.

Tom jammed his hands in his coat pockets, and she saw him clench them underneath the material. Was he cold? Or was something else going on? The night was a little chilly, but fairly mild in the grand scheme of impending winter.

Certainly not too cold for a goodnight kiss. She leaned forward, puckered her lips, lowered her eyelids, and waited.

Kiss me, kiss me, kiss me.

He did not.

Slowly, she opened her eyes, unpuckered her lips, and felt disappointment roll through her in one long wave, starting at her feet and sweeping up to her heart, gathering heat as it went until it lodged in her head as a hot, throbbing frustration.

"See you on Saturday," he mumbled and with a quick, but really weird salute, he dashed back to his car.

Leaving Jude perplexed and wanting more. So very much more.

Why didn't you tell him that?

Why? Because she was afraid that he'd tell her she was "too nice" to be his girlfriend. Although, she did have a counter for that argument. She wasn't asking to be his girlfriend. All she wanted was a temporary bed partner.

But saying that required bravery and boldness.

If you want to be bold, the only way to get there is to act boldly.

Next time, if Tom didn't make a move, she was kissing him, and this time, it would darn well be on the lips.

THE WEEK WAS BUSY, AND BY THURSDAY, JUDE WAS aching for a fun-filled Saturday night, but for the life of her, she couldn't cook up an adequate adventure for her date with Tom.

It's not a date, she reminded herself. He was merely giving her some pointers on navigating the dating world. They were just friends. She'd come to this conclusion after he'd taken off without even trying to kiss her the other evening.

She hadn't heard from him all week. Not that she

expected to. C'mon, she wasn't that needy, but she had thought maybe he'd at least drop her a text.

Nope. Nothing.

And she was cool with that. Totally.

The last school bell had rang and she was tidying up the library when she felt someone stroll up behind her. Thinking it was one of the students returning for a lost cell phone or book bag, she didn't even look up from what she was doing.

Until a masculine voice cut through her distractions. "Hey, Jude."

A sweet shiver went up her spine as she turned to see Tom standing there with an inviting lopsided grin, humming the iconic Beatles song for which she'd been named.

"How did you get in here?" she asked. "Our school has tight security."

"I'm on the list."

"What list?" she asked, confused.

"My nephew goes here. He's a freshman and he doesn't drive yet, so my sister put me on the pickup list just in case."

"Tara has a son old enough to be in high school?"

"No, not Tara, my half sister, Mica."

"I didn't know you had a half sister."

"She's ten years older and a result of my father's misspent youth before he met my mom. I didn't even know about Mica until fifteen years ago. She came looking for us after she found out who her father was through a DNA test. She's a single mom and needs all the help she can get, so I do what I can. Plus, I enjoy hanging out with my nephew. He's a good kid."

Aww, that was sweet of Tom to help out a half sister he hadn't known for a big chunk of his life.

"Oh, wow. Who's your nephew?"

"Joe Brown."

Jude crinkled her nose and tried to place the student, but it was a common name and twelve hundred students went to the high school. Tom's nephew must have been in the library at some point, but she didn't know him.

"So since you can get into the building, you thought you'd just pop on over to the library to see what I was up to?" With a book in her hand, she folded her arms over her chest. It was chilly at this end of the building, and well, her bra was thin.

"Something like that." An amused smile overtook his face. "Joe had a dental appointment this morning and Mica had to be at work, and since I'm my own boss, I came over. I brought Joe back from his appointment in time to catch the last class of the day and..."

"And?" She arched an eyebrow.

"I stuck around until school was out so I could talk to you."

"You've been hanging around for an hour?"

"The day was pretty well shot for getting anything done, so I listened to an audiobook in the car."

"What book?" she asked, feeling certain he was going to name the latest New York Times bestseller, but he surprised her.

"*East of Eden*."

"Really?" That reply tickled her no end. "Steinbeck?"

"You say that as if I'm some knuckle-dragging caveman who's lucky to read my car repair manual."

"No, no." She shook her head and waved a hand. "Not at all. I just didn't picture you reading...Steinbeck."

"Why not?"

"I love Steinbeck," she said. "But I find few people nowadays who still read him."

"Well," he said. "Now you've found somebody."

"That is..." She paused, feeling an uptick in her pulse and no decent explanation for it. "Unexpected."

"Truth?" he said.

"Always."

"I'm on a self-improvement kick and reading the classics is part of that plan."

"Ooh," she said, intrigued. "It's good to know I'm

not the only one trying to transform. I'd like to hear more about that."

His grin was as warm as a flannel blanket. "It's not that impressive. I just regularly seek out ways to hone my competitive edge. Reading does that for me, as does vigorous exercise, Tai Chi, and meditation. I'm all about constant, never-ending improvement."

She liked that sentiment, because Jude too love learning. It's why she had a master's degree in library science. Commitment to continuing education was something she hadn't expected them to have in common.

Captivated, she sent a lingering glance over his body. "Nourish the body and the mind."

"The two do go hand-in-hand."

"They do," she echoed.

"Maybe we could take a class together sometime," he said.

"I'd like that." She paused. "Very much."

His dark eyes captured hers and the back of her knees tingled. Then he glanced around the room, taking in the books, desks, and Thanksgiving decorations. "So this is your home away from home."

She could look into his eyes for infinity and never get bored. Scary thought, that. She clutched tightly to the book she was still holding to her chest, using it as a shield against the intensity of her burgeoning feelings.

Oh, there was chemistry here. Lots of it.

While the air smoldered between them, she entertained images of kissing him until neither of them could breathe, tearing off his clothes, pulling him to the floor between the bookshelves—

Whoa! What was wrong with her?

The book stacks were sacred, and here she was thinking of desecrating them in a wholly inappropriate way with Tom Brunswick.

Her cell phone rang.

Thank God!

Eager to derail her crazy fantasies, she snatched the phone up from her desk and answered without even registering who was calling.

❧

"Oh, Dirk, hello," Jude purred into her cell phone.

Every muscle in Tom's body tensed. His college buddy was at it again, trying to stir Tom's jealousy. *Be rational. Dirk doesn't know you're here.* Which was actually worse. It meant Dirk might truly be interested in Jude for himself.

Jude looked at Tom, smiled, and shrugged. "Yes, yes, I agree."

What was she agreeing with? Tom wanted to jerk the phone from her hand and hang up on Dirk. Of course, he wouldn't do that. She had a right to talk to Dirk if she wanted, but he didn't have to like it.

Tom jammed his hands into his pockets and paced a small circle around the library as Jude laughed gaily at something Dirk said.

His buddy was a funny guy. Tom had to admit that. When Dirk pulled out all the stops on his charm, women fell at his feet.

Scowling, Tom hauled in a deep breath. *Steady.* Being jealous played right into Dirk's scheme. The man played to win. Always.

Yeah, well, so did Tom.

Even though he hated the idea of using Jude as a pawn in their power play, Dirk clearly did not, and he wasn't going to let the son of a gun hurt her.

"Tonight?" Jude's voice went up a note.

Tom stopped pacing and swung his head around to study her.

"That's short notice," she went on, not noticing that Tom was noticing her. Then she laughed again. "Yes, you're right. *Carpe noctem,* seize the night as if there were no tomorrow."

Tom waved his arms to get her attention.

"Hang on a minute, Dirk." Jude muted her conversation and gave Tom her full attention. "What is it?"

"Did Dirk just ask you out for tonight?" he asked.

"He did."

"And you're considering going?"

She gave him a half-smile as if enjoying his discomfort. "I am."

"Don't go," Tom blurted.

"Why not?"

"Because *I* came to ask you out for tonight." When he'd dropped by to see her, he'd had no intention of inviting her to the family gathering where he was headed this evening—his aunt's sixtieth birthday celebration.

"You did?"

Immediately, the impact of his invitation hit Tom. He would essentially be taking her to meet his family. Awk-*ward*!

"Yep." He bit off the 'p' at the last minute, dithering, and it came out on a puff of air.

She angled him an odd look as if she were trying to read his mind. "Hang on a minute."

"Huh?"

She unmuted her phone and said to Dirk, "I'm sorry I can't tonight." Jude paused and met Tom's gaze. "No, I'm afraid I have plans for Saturday night too."

With him. *Ha, Poomph! Take that.*

"Tomorrow? Bowling? Why, yes, I am free tomorrow night to go bowling."

Tom grimaced. Was she seriously going out with Dirk?

"I do have to warn you that I used to bowl in a league," she told Dirk. "Oh, you like competition? Be careful what you wish for; you just might get it."

Could Dirk actually be serious about Jude? That thought did nothing to boost his mood.

"Sure. Seven thirty sounds good. See you then." She disconnected and slipped the phone into her pocket.

Hungrily, Tom watched her graceful movements as her hands fluttered to her hips and her chin tilted down as she eyed him speculatively.

"You're going out with Dirk?" he asked.

She shrugged. "Sure. Why not? The best way to get over a broken heart is to get back out there, right?"

"Um...I suppose." He didn't like this at all. "What about the other guy you were telling me about?"

"Oh, him." She waved a hand. "You were right. If he can't take me as I am, who needs him?"

Yes! One less guy vying for her attention.

"I've got to know one thing, though."

"What's that?" Tom asked, distracted. Her scent was tangled up in his head like fishing line.

"Why?"

"Why what?"

"Why are you asking me out now? You could have called any time this week. You could have texted. Instead, you show up at my place of work for a spur of the moment invitation. I want to know why."

Tom squirmed. He didn't want to answer that direct question, so he said, "I need a date for my Aunt Pru's sixtieth birthday party tonight. You might have seen her at the wedding. She was one of my mother's three sisters."

"I met so many people that night, I'm afraid I sorted your mother's sisters out by dress color. Puce, coral, and chartreuse. Which one was she?"

He couldn't be expected to notice what his aunts wore and what color was puce anyway? "She's the tallest. Has a gap between her two front teeth."

"Chartreuse."

"Um...if you say so."

"So you had a birthday party planned and you're just now asking me to go with you?" She looked a little miffed, her hands moving up from her hips to fold across her chest.

"I—"

"Did your original date stand you up?"

Oh, thanks for the excuse. Although the conclusion she'd jumped to didn't cast him in such a great light, he nodded. Okay, it was a little white lie, but he hadn't actually said yes. Would she lower the boom on him for not asking her sooner?

To his surprise, she too nodded. "I understand. Getting stood up really hurts."

Ouch. He stepped on a sore spot.

Tom had never been dumped so he couldn't speak to that, but he did have a few choice words for the jerk who'd treated Jude so shabbily. He wanted to draw her into his arms and hold her tight and tell her no one would ever hurt her again. But then that thought scared him, so he stuffed it way down inside.

"You'll come with me?" He gave her a boyish grin and a half shrug.

"Will your sister Mica be there?" she asked. "And Joe?"

"Other side of the family," he said.

She touched her chin with her fingers and looked pensive.

Say no, say no, say no, he prayed. His family would read all kinds of things into it if he brought Jude to the birthday party.

"Sure," she said. "Why not? I don't have anything

else planned for the evening. See? I can be sponta-neous and fun."

"That's terrific," he said, not meaning it. Why had he started on this course of action in the first place?

Oh yeah. Dirk. He didn't want to give that scoundrel an inch. Tom knew far too well how his buddy maneuvered.

"Are you ready to go?" he asked.

"Now?"

"The party's at six and it's across town. We need to leave now if we want to beat the traffic."

"I should go home and change—"

"You look perfect." And she did in that smart black turtleneck sweater and red plaid skirt with black leggings and fashion boots. "Besides, the party is 'come as you are.'"

"Where does your aunt live exactly?"

"About half an hour west. Are you ready to go?"

"Won't it be way out of your way to bring me here afterward for my car?"

"I don't mind."

"How about this? I'll follow you."

"That's not necessary. I don't mind coming back this way."

"Hey, it's not a real date, right?" She laughed. "I'm just filling in for the one who stood you up."

She had him there, caught in his white lie.

"No, no," he mumbled. "Of course not."

"All right, then." She rubbed her palms together and grinned. "Let's do this thing. I'll just grab my coat."

While she went to the cubby, he quickly texted his mom and told her he was bringing Jude to the birthday party. Mom replied with a string of emojis signifying she was thrilled by his news.

"Ready," Jude said, coming to stand beside him. She was bundled up in that cute white ski jacket of hers, and they walked side by side to his Mustang in the almost empty high school parking lot.

What was he getting himself into, taking Jude to a family gathering again so soon in their relationship?

Relationship?

He was officially losing his marbles. They barely knew each other. He was just trying to keep her safe from Dirk.

Sure, tell yourself pretty stories.

Okay, he liked her. Not against the law.

He pressed a palm to his forehead and watched her walk as she headed to the passenger side, stepping agilely around patches of ice. She had a deliciously cute fanny, one that he yearned to cup.

Sprinting to beat her to the passenger door so he could open it for her, Tom slipped on the ice and busted his ass. His legs went out from under him and his arms windmilled and *splat*.

"Oh! Oh!" Jude exclaimed, crouching beside him where he lay on the asphalt, staring up at her.

God, she had such gorgeous blue eyes.

"Are you all right? What did you hurt?"

"My pride," he said, springing to his feet.

"Are you sure?" Frowning, she straightened and looked concerned.

"A little humiliation never killed anyone," he quipped, dusting off his clothes.

"You don't have to play the chivalrous knight for me," she said. "I can open my own car door."

"Got it." He opened the door for her anyway.

Chuckling, she climbed inside.

"What can I say?" he asked, overwhelmed at the scholarly scent of her perfume. The woman was intoxicating, and she was just so down-to-earth.

As they pulled into traffic, Tom wondered again if taking Jude to see his family was a big mistake. She was the kind of woman you brought home to mother. His folks were bound to read things into it.

On the drive over, he filled Jude in about his relatives, picking upbeat, jovial stories to tell her, and she seemed honestly interested.

Upon arrival at his aunt and uncle's home, he told her that his aunt Prudence and her husband Horace

—since his fiftieth birthday, he preferred to be called Bud, but no one in the family remembered—had bought a small ranch style house early in their marriage and spent over thirty years embellishing it. Aluminum awnings hung in odd spots, and flower boxes with dead stalks had hearts cut into them. The walk was a maze of leafless hedges, cement garden ornaments, and big flower tubs now dormant.

He guided Jude to the front door with his hand lightly at her waist, his whole arm vibrating because her walk felt as good as it looked.

The door flew open before they could ring the bell—his aunt's radar in action. He must have been out of his mind bringing Jude here.

His mom and her sisters swooped down on Jude the instant they stepped inside, welcoming her as if she were a long-lost relative—or the woman destined to drag a happy bachelor to his Waterloo.

"Welcome, welcome," Aunt Pru gushed and waved them inside. "Come meet everyone. We're tickled pink to see you again, Jude."

Tom reluctantly trailed behind her even though he wanted to bolt. He couldn't desert her while she ran the family gauntlet.

"Of course, I remember you," Jude said to his Aunt Susan. "You were wearing that lovely coral dress at the wedding."

"Come, come," said Aunt Cathy. "All the action is in the kitchen."

His aunts beamed. They liked Jude.

He groaned inwardly, wondering what it was about her that brought out his protective urges, and boy, did he wish that was the only urge she inspired.

Forbidden fruit, he thought unhappily. Just because he'd taken a celibacy challenge didn't mean he could stop thinking about her in a wholly sexual way. He caught a glimpse of her perfect breasts under a soft black sweater and had to wipe his sweaty palms on the sides of his jeans.

She wasn't the most beautiful woman he'd ever dated, but she was just so damn cute. Pert and bright and friendly, and watching her mingle with his family, she seemed to grow more lovely before his eyes.

Slow down, Brunswick. You're just sex-starved.

Jude was gorgeous, but she was on the rebound. She was in a place where she needed to cut loose and do crazy things for once in her life, and he wasn't going to be the one to take advantage of that vulnerability.

No, but Dirk might.

That thought had him gritting his teeth.

"Put your tongue back in your mouth, dummy!" His cousin Biff—Pru and Horace's oldest son who ran a construction crew—came up behind him, swatted

Tom's arm with one hand, and gestured with a big chunk of Italian bread in the other. "Everyone will see how much you want her, and then they'll start planning your wedding."

"What are you talking about?"

"The happy day when you have to eat crow for all your footloose and fancy-free bachelor manifesto." Biff guffawed like he'd told a hilarious joke.

"Haven't you put on a few pounds?" Tom teased good-naturedly, attempting to change the subject. "Shouldn't you be holed up somewhere making a baby with your new wife instead of chowing down with the relatives?"

"Deflection," Biff announced. "Not gonna work with me."

Tom looked around, realizing Biff backed him into the little alcove Horace—er, Bud—had built to display his first, and only, bowling trophy. Now it was a bower of shelves filled with glass baskets and his aunt's collection of British royal family memorabilia, all lit by dazzling overhead lights.

"I'm only helping her out. Jude's got self-esteem issues after her ex-fiancé dumped her at the altar."

"So you're like what? The rebound guy?"

"We're not having sex."

"Maybe not yet." Biff waggled his eyebrows. "But

it's on the table. She was looking at you with as much sizzle as you were looking at her."

Was she?

Tom felt proud...and worried. "I'd better go rescue Jude before Uncle Ray starts doing his ear-wiggling trick."

Leaving his cousin behind, Tom practically sprinted to the kitchen where his aunts had absconded with Jude.

9

"My aunts are terrific cooks," Tom whispered to Jude when they were seated side by side at the long dinner table. "Their menus can be a little strange—all three are uber-creative—but I promise everything tastes good."

Jude didn't mind. She found his boisterous family quite interesting, and she'd been enjoying their conversations where they talked over each other, interrupted often, and laughed with abandon. By comparison, her own family was much more placid.

Tom ladled some pickled beets and a big purple egg onto his plate beside the main dish of meatballs and spaghetti. Not a combo she would have served, but hey, she was open to new experiences.

He winked at her. Luckily, his family was deeply

engaged in their reminiscing about past birthday celebrations that they didn't notice what was going on at Tom and Jude's end of the table.

Jude eyed Tom with a speculative smile. "Does your family have a lot of these kinds of celebrations?"

"Oh, yeah. At least once a month someone is having a birthday or getting promoted or having a baby or graduating. We keep the party supply store in business."

"I think that's sweet," Jude said. "It's nice having a big extended family close by. You're lucky."

"It can be annoying too," he confessed. "When they decide to get all up in your business."

"Oops," Jude murmured. "I dropped my napkin."

"I'll get it," he said, but playing Sir Galahad wasn't as easy as he made it sound.

For one thing, Tom's aunt had put extra leaves in her dining room table, and too many folding chairs were crowded around it, so he bumped into people as he maneuvered. For another thing, with a wall behind them, he could wiggle back only a couple of inches, and he had to bend his body at an odd angle to peek beneath the tablecloth for her errant napkin.

He ducked his head and reached down.

Jude felt fingers against her skin, and she jumped at his touch. Her pulse rate scooted upward, and she hissed softly, "That's my shin."

He rooted around, then came up for air, his face flushed and hair tousled. "Sorry. I couldn't find it. You can have mine."

"Let's share. Your aunt's napkins are as big as bedsheets." Jude chuckled.

"Thank you for being so gracious and understanding," he whispered close to her ear, although it was unlikely anyone could hear him. It took a top-of-the-lungs shout to be heard across the table in the din of several dozen people talking at once. "Would you like to leave as soon as we have cake and ice cream?"

"No, I'm having fun," she said.

"Really?" Tom looked surprised.

Even as she said it, Jude realized it was true. Her family was smaller and widely scattered. Tom's relatives talked too loudly, laughed a lot, and seemed genuinely fond of each other. They also made her, a stranger, feel welcome and liked.

But they kept talking about the happy marriages among their clan and eying Jude with curiosity. She could see their mental gears clicking—especially with Tom's mother—wondering if Jude might be the one to tame him.

Ha! The last thing she wanted was a serious relationship. With Tom, all Jude wanted was fun, fun, fun, fun.

She liked him and enjoyed being around him, but

that was the extent of it. She was glad she'd accepted Dirk's invitation to go bowling tomorrow night, although she got the feeling Tom disapproved. She needed to play the field. Not that she was dating Tom or anything, but the more time she spent with him, the more she was getting attached to his quick smile and lively nature.

"A toast," Uncle Horace/Bud proposed, lifting a precariously full goblet of red wine. "To my better half. I love you, Prudie!"

Horace was as verbose as he was jolly. He kept the toasts going, jumping in whenever there was a lull. Which granted, with this bunch, wasn't often.

Jude nursed one glass of wine last through ten rounds of toasting and glass-clinking, but the bright lights from the chandelier and the close-packed bodies were making a steam room of the dining area.

When the meal was over and the birthday cake eaten, a few people drifted away from the table, and Tom was quick to lead her away from the dining room hullabaloo. Jude followed, squeezing behind the chairs hemming them in.

When he put his hand on her upper arm, she pulled away. They were surrounded by a hoard of his relatives, including his mother, and she was literally vibrating with—

Call it what it is, she chided.

Desire.

Somehow, they ended up in the kitchen alone. The counter was crowded with more small electrical kitchen aids than she'd ever seen outside of a store.

Tom read her mind. "Uncle Horace is big on mechanical gadgets. If Aunt Pru got anything else for Christmas or her birthday, she'd probably faint."

Jude stared at the collection of dicers, slicers, cookers, toasters, beaters, heaters, and others with mysterious purposes.

"Why three microwaves?"

"In case two malfunction." He grinned. "Aunt Pru is serious about cuisine."

"No kidding."

"Let's see if we can find a quiet corner somewhere in the house."

"To talk." She was telling herself, not him.

He led the way down red-tiled steps to the basement, but here, too, every inch seemed to be living space. The rec room had a bar and a ping-pong table, both already in use. Tom led her through a second boxy room, a sewing niche it appeared, and opened a closed door, only to find two carrot-headed cousins playing a video game in another paneled, carpeted room.

Tom bribed them to leave with two ten-dollar bills.

"My," she said as the boys darted for the door. "You do have a way with kids."

"Money talks." He laughed.

"You have an entertaining family."

"Please..." He rolled his eyes.

"No, I mean it." She sat on a threadbare couch, pretending to study the old neon signs hanging on knotty-pine walls.

"They're wacky."

"They seem completely normal to me."

"Oh, just wait, you haven't heard all the stories yet."

He said it as if she'd be sticking around, and that pulled her in two different directions. The Jude that wanted to hang out with Tom and his family and the Jude who knew it was better for her personal development to play the field right now. Which was why she'd said yes when Dirk asked her to go bowling, but she was already wishing she hadn't committed.

"Somehow I get the impression there's not many skeletons in your family's closet," she said.

"We do tend to let it all hang out."

"My kind of folk."

Their eyes met and her heart did a swoony little dance that left her thinking, *Good thing I said yes to Dirk. Gotta do something to break Tom's spell.*

That said, once she'd played the field awhile, she

wouldn't mind finding someone to settle down with —*eventually*. Especially if he was as cute as Tom. Although, eventually Mr. Right didn't have to have unruly dark hair that invited finger-combing or brown eyes that turned her knees to water, but she did love Brunswick's legs.

She could see the swell of muscle in his calf when he rested one ankle on his other knee, and his thighs looked strong and firm in jeans that fit like a second skin. And when he reached over to touch her knee, she melted like chocolate in the sun.

"Listen," he said. "I should warn you about Dirk."

Hmm, was that jealousy she heard in his voice? "Warn? He's not a good guy? I thought he was your friend."

"He is, but you gotta accept people as they are, right?"

"What are you trying to say?" she mumbled, her gaze fixed on his broad fingers resting on her knee. Underneath her leggings, little flames spread heat up her thigh.

"I don't want you to go out with Dirk."

"Because he's a bad person?"

"No," Tom said. "Because..."

Jude ticked the lock on their fused gazes, drilling down to the core of the man through his pupils. "Because what?"

He gulped.

Was Tom about to say he didn't want her to date his buddy because *he* wanted to date her? Jude held her breath, crossed her fingers, and waited. Hoped.

He squirmed.

"Well?"

"Dirk's a player. That doesn't make him a bad guy; it's just who he is."

"And you're not a player?" She wrinkled her forehead.

"No."

"You're thirty and have never been married."

"So?"

"Some people might say that's an indication that *you* can't commit."

"What people?" He narrowed his eyes and lowered his grin, but she could see amusement dancing at the corners of his mouth.

"Your aunts and your mother. You forget, you left me alone with them for all of ten minutes. Now I know everything about you."

He looked unnerved by that comment. "I'm just saying, around Dirk, guard your heart."

"Maybe he should guard his." Jude tossed her head. "I'm getting in touch with my wild side, remember?"

Tom's mouth completely flattened, and his pupils

rounded in what looked a lot like dismay. He was *sooo* jealous of Dirk, but she had a feeling the jealousy went beyond Dirk's interest in her. *Hmm*. What was that all about?

"Maybe he should," Tom said.

Maybe I should guard my heart, Jude thought. *With you.* "Tell me what's going on between you and Dirk?"

Tom took his hand back and settled deeper into his seat. "What are you talking about?"

"I'm beginning to feel like a yo-yo between you two. As if I'm being used to settle some old score."

His eyelids flew all the way open. "Um..."

"Your reaction says it all. So what's the deal? I don't mind if you're using me to work something out with your buddy; I just need to know that."

He moistened his lips, chuffed out a breath, and said, "Dirk stole my first real girlfriend during our sophomore year of college."

"A decade ago?"

He dipped his head and when he spoke, he sounded chagrinned. "We were roommates. He knew I was head over heels for Amanda."

"And you've never forgiven him?"

"We're very competitive with each other."

"I'm listening."

"Some people might say our competitiveness borders on a sickness."

LORI WILDE & & PAM ANDREWS HANSON

"What people?"

"My aunts and mother." He grinned.

"You do understand by warning me off Dirk and his competitiveness that you're warning me off you as well."

Tom sighed. "Yeah, I get that."

"But you'd rather Dirk *not* have me, than for you *to* have me."

"No, wait. What?" He scratched his head and looked totally confused.

"Look," she said. "If you want me to help you get back at Dirk so you can move on from your heartbreak, I will."

"You will?"

She shrugged. "It's time you let go of ancient history, Tom. You're stuck in the past. You've got to move on. Believe me, that's why I wanted you to help me not be so nice. I don't want to end up like you."

"Wh-what?" Tom stammered.

"Jaxon might have broken my heart, but I don't want to spend the next decade resenting him the way you resent Dirk. It's time you let Amanda go."

"I've let her go."

"No, you haven't. If you had, you wouldn't be so obsessed with your buddy."

"Maybe."

"What happened to Amanda?" she asked, honestly curious.

"Dirk dumped her like a hot potato as soon as he'd won her away from me. She's married now to a good guy who treats her right. They live in Colorado and have three boys. We exchange Christmas cards. I'm happy for her."

He didn't seem to be pining for his lost love at all and that was encouraging. He'd managed to act like a mature adult with Amanda, even if he hadn't gotten there with Dirk. The issue *did* seem to be his rivalry with his friend.

"Why are you still friends with him?" she asked. "After the way he treated you?"

Tom shrugged. "He's fun. He has good taste in microbreweries, and I can beat him at basketball."

"You have a pretty low bar for friendships."

"What can I say?" Tom chuckled. "I'm easygoing."

"An easygoing competitive person?" She shook her head. "Not buying it."

"It's true."

"Well, since most of your family seems to be here, maybe I should ask go them what they think?"

He measured off an inch with his finger and thumb. "Maybe I do have a little bit of an issue with competition."

"Do you want to know what I think?"

Tom moved closer. "I'm listening."

"You stay friends with Dirk because you enjoy the conflict."

Tom shook his head. "No."

"Yes." Jude nodded. "You do."

"Do I?"

"You're not very self-aware, are you?"

"Hey!" he exclaimed, but he was smiling. She hadn't offended him. "I resemble that remark."

She laughed.

He sobered. "Look, there's something I need to come clean about."

"Oh?"

"It's the real reason Dirk asked you out."

"You mean his invitation to go bowling has more to do with him trying to steal away the woman he thinks you're interested in rather than in my beauty and charm?"

"You," he said, "are sharp as a tack."

His compliment lit her up inside. *Don't let flattery go to your head.*

"Thank you," she said. "Part of being nice comes from being observant and trying to understand what makes other people tick."

"So now that you know Dirk's interest in you isn't serious, you'll cancel the date?" He sounded optimistic.

"No way."

Tom blinked. "No? Why not?"

"Because I don't want to date someone who wants to get serious. I just want to have a good time."

"I can show you a good time," he offered, sliding even closer to her on the couch and slipping his arm around her shoulders.

"What are you doing?" she asked, equal parts charmed and alarmed. Suddenly her pulse was galloping like a Thoroughbred racehorse.

The overhead lights flickered once, then again. "Horace needs to rewire the basement," Tom muttered. "I'll bet—"

This time the lights flickered and went out. The windowless room was doused in darkness. They heard a few muted sounds in the space beyond, but the door shut them off from the people in the rec room.

"Where's the switch box?" she asked, instinctively standing even though it didn't seem wise to stumble around in an unfamiliar dark basement.

"Probably in the furnace area. Someone will take care of it."

She hadn't realized how close he was, and she found his nearness exciting.

"A bold woman would know what to do now," he said in a husky voice she hadn't heard before.

"Turn on the flashlight feature on her phone?"

"I was thinking along the lines of something wilder."

She reached out and let her hand rest on his chest, hearing and feeling his sharp intake of breath and the steady lub-dub of his heart. "You're saying that in a blackout a bold woman would take advantage of the situation to indulge her romantic needs?"

"That's one option," he whispered.

She could feel his breath on her forehead, and then his lips were there, kissing her dead center between the eyebrows.

"Why are you kissing my forehead?" she challenged brazenly. She moistened her lips with the tip of her tongue, then leaned toward him just as his arms circled her, his fingers caressing her back, inching up her sweater.

"Oh..."

His mouth covered hers. She parted her lips, ignoring all the reasons why this was a bad idea, but he tasted so darn good, she thought, *screw it* and drew him down on top of her.

10

Tom was breaking all the rules of their bar bet. This was definitely the beginning of sexual activity, and he was still over a month away from winning the wager.

But Dirk had gotten inside his head and eroded Tom's self-control.

C'mon. Jude was a pretty hot tamale and she was kissing him with as much fervor as he was kissing her. This had nothing to do with Dirk.

He'd been on the verge of telling her about the bet when the lights went out, but now his mind was on one thing.

The sweet heat of her lips and the softness of her skin beneath his palms. All his preconceived theories about Jude were dying like burnt-out sparklers.

There was nothing he could teach her about

fitting her body to his, rubbing against him in a dozen different places, all of them insanely erotic. He felt like a superhero breaking free of a hundred ropes binding his body.

She was the aggressor now, nipping at his lips between breathless little kisses, running her hands over the front of his shirt until she found and teased his nipples through the cloth.

"Oh..." His moan welled up, and he ached with hard need.

"We shouldn't..." she murmured.

"No, not here, you're right."

"Tom..."

The lights came on, harsh and sudden.

They blinked at each other. Her lips were swollen, her eyes wide as a baby deer's.

"I've got to go." She shoved him aside and sprang to her feet, surprising him with the strength behind her panicky retreat.

"Okay, okay." He jammed his fingers through his hair and realized that somewhere along the way she'd started to unbutton his shirt. Swiftly, he buttoned up. "I'll drive you back to school to get your car."

"No! I'll call for an Uber." She turned and ran, leaving the door open behind her, sprinting away with the speed of a frightened rabbit.

So much for being a bold woman, he thought with a

mixture of amusement and regret, in no state to rush after her through a bunch of curious relatives.

How would she handle herself on her date with Dirk if a few kisses spooked her enough to turn tail? Of course, he was the one who should be running as far away from Jude Bailey as he could get. He hadn't gotten so hard and hot so quickly in ages—*if ever*.

Breathing deeply, he tried to think sobering thoughts and forget the impact she'd had on him. He had a bet to win.

And he had to find a way to keep Jude safe from Dirk in the process.

❧❧❧

"THINK ABOUT *DIRK, DIRK, DIRK*," JUDE CHANTED.

She felt like a witch casting a spell, but the only one she was trying to enchant was herself—Jude Bailey, single working woman, on a mission to have fun and not start anything serious with anyone.

This wasn't her usual way of psyching herself up for a first date, but she was having a hard time remembering what Dirk looked like. His image drifted somewhere in the fog-shrouded recesses of her mind, but when she tried to focus on it, he came through with Tom's face.

It was all Brunswick's fault—well, mostly his fault.

Okay, partly his fault. A man whose kisses had real oomph—not Dirk-Poomph-oomph—shouldn't scatter them around like unguided missiles.

She pressed a palm against her mouth, in her mind erasing the sweetly sensual sensation of his lips on hers.

It was hopeless. The only way she was going to get Tom out of her mind was to have a wonderful time with Dirk. She didn't care about their ridiculous rivalry. It was prideful male posturing and that was between them.

Jude was determined to have as much fun as possible—*if* she ever made up her mind what to wear. She wanted to set the right tone. She glanced at the nightstand clock as she sat on the edge of the bed, struggling to make her leggings go up smoothly over slightly damp legs.

They were going to dinner first. Dinner was nice. She wasn't familiar with the restaurant where Dirk had made reservations, but Misty Shores Inn suggested candlelight and romantic music and she was down for that.

She slipped into her best bra, leaning over to fill the cups before hooking it closed in back. Why was she getting ready so early? Something about a last-minute rush always pumped her up for a terrific date —or a terrible one.

Now she was probably going to be ready too early, and that meant pacing and waiting, letting doubts grow. She was horrible at dating, which was why she'd been so relieved when Jaxon had proposed.

That thought hit her hard.

Wow, was *that* why she'd said yes to Jaxon? Because he'd asked and she'd been tired of dating? But no, surely not. Jaxon was handsome and had a very muscular body and the deepest hazel eyes, and OMG, she totally had!

Jude placed a hand on her forehead. If it was true that only Jaxon's looks, body, and availability had wrangled her into an engagement, she better darn well get her priorities straight before jumping into another relationship.

Thank heavens Jaxon *had* dumped her at the altar. She'd be married to him now if he hadn't.

What a mistake that would have been.

For the first time since the botched wedding, Jude raised her eyes heavenward and whispered, "Thank you."

That realization didn't make first dates easier. Jude peered at herself in the mirror. Her long dark hair was still slightly damp, but she brushed it into the smooth style that framed her face in what her mother called her "Botticelli look." She wasn't big on heavy makeup; mascara and a trace of eye shadow, plus lipstick, did it for her. She applied her favorite cherry-red lip gloss, bright and slightly daring, and wondered if Tom would call it a color that bold women wore.

Damn! Why did Tom Brunswick keep popping into her head?

She checked her makeup one more time, dabbed cologne on her throat, earlobes, and the hollow between her breasts, and then hoped she hadn't overdone it.

In a decisive mood now, she finished dressing for a night at the bowling alley. A pullover sweater and a short skirt for ease of movement, with leggings underneath. Nothing sexy about the outfit. It was much like her everyday work attire. She needed something to elevate the look. What shoes should she wear?

She studied her labeled shoeboxes on the closet shelf. How tall was Dirk?

She tried to remember dancing with him, but when she looked up in her daydream, her imagery dance partner always had Tom's slightly crooked smile and warm brown eyes.

"When in doubt go low." She chose her simple one-inch black pumps, not that she was tall, but her dressy three-inch spikes might make her as tall as Dirk, and she didn't want to wear anything that would make him feel uncomfortable.

And when Dirk showed up, all smooth toothy smiles, slicked-back hair, and smelling of island breezes, standing just a few inches taller than she, Jude was very glad she'd gone for the short pumps.

Dirk overdid the compliments, but Jude accepted them graciously. She planned to have a great evening, and that meant forgetting about Tom.

"I made reservations for seven thirty," her date reminded her unnecessarily.

He had a young voice, or maybe it was a little high for a man. It reminded her of the awkward adolescents who'd showed up in her library every day. This guy bugged Tom?

Jude didn't understand it. In her mind, Dirk had nothing on Tom.

"I'm ready," she assured Dirk. "We won't be late."

She quickly grabbed her nice coat, slipping into it before Dirk could help her.

Dirk was at least three inches shorter than Tom, but what he lacked in height, he made up for with charisma and good looks—cracking self-deprecating jokes, making firm eye contact, but not holding her gaze long enough to become creepy.

With her low heels they stood eyeball-to-eyeball, but that didn't prejudice her against him. Size was no

LORI WILDE & & PAM ANDREWS HANSON

biggie. There was a natural curl in his professionally styled russet-colored hair, and he had the cutest dimples. He wore creased khaki slacks and a white polo shirt. His style was understated preppie.

Not her usual type, but neither was Tom.

In the parking lot, Dirk took her arm so she wouldn't slip on an icy patch, then opened the door of his new model Audi for her and she caught herself thinking of Tom's vintage Mustang. She did remember that Dirk had a good sense of humor and wore a spicy aftershave with hints of anise. This promised to be a great first date if she could stop thinking about Tom and his rivalry with the man beside her.

Giving Dirk the benefit of the doubt, Jude threw herself into her role as a charming companion. She remembered Tom's warning against Dirk, but she was a big girl, and she could take care of herself.

Dirk made it easy for her to be congenial— opening doors, helping with her coat, pulling out her chair, just like Tom did. She was able to sit back and let him do all the work. All she had to do was remain alluring and mysterious.

Their waiter was tall and broad-shouldered. He probably made great tips at the upscale restaurant, but he took his job a little too seriously, hovering over them while they tasted the wine and sampled their appetizers. He wore his hair in a tail, and she wondered if Tom's shaggy hair style was long enough to tie back. Probably not, but their waiter had long legs and a tight, muscular butt that reminded her so strongly of Tom she had to study her place setting whenever he turned his back to the table.

Damn you, Tom Brunswick! she thought with a flash of anger. Why couldn't she get the man off her mind?

It was all Brunswick's fault that she wasn't enjoying a pleasant date with a fascinating guy who wasn't afraid of showing he was interested in a woman. She didn't want to be thinking of Tom while Dirk was working hard to entertain her.

She owed him her full attention and Jude tried harder to follow the gist of his stories. Maybe this was what marriage was all about: being a sounding board, a good listener, and supportive of your partner. But she wanted more from life than meeting everyone else's needs and she hadn't even realized it until Jaxon dumped her. She wanted excitement, challenges, breathless romance. Completely against her will, she conjured up an image of Tom as Zorro— one of her go-to sexual fantasies—stripped bare to the waist, grinning widely with a dueling sword in hand.

Ack! Stop it.

"And we all had a good laugh over that," Dirk said,

concluding a story.

Guiltily, she smiled broadly, trying to make up for missing the tale that preceded the punchline. He chuckled and looked as if he thought she might laugh too. Jude gave a little haha and hoped she got away with her poor listening skills. He couldn't expect her to roar with laughter over the antics of people she didn't know.

Jude focused on appreciating the meal. Her fresh salmon, poached in cream, was the best thing she'd eaten in weeks. The food was absolutely delicious and served with elegant flair.

When Dirk went into raptures over the dessert cart, she gave him the go-ahead to order a slice of raspberry cheesecake for them to share.

"We'll burn off the calories on the lanes," he promised.

They polished off the cheesecake—Dirk let her have the last bite—and then he said, "Jude, there's a reason I asked you out tonight beyond the fact you're a captivating woman."

"Oh?" She blinked, feeling a little blindsided.

"With that in mind, I have an interesting proposition for you."

Without missing a beat, the emerging wild woman inside her said, "Bring it."

No harm in letting the man ask for what he

wanted, was there? She didn't have to say yes.

"WHAT'S WITH THE SUDDEN URGE TO BOWL?" BUCK Kelly, Tom's warehouse foreman, asked that same evening as they headed to Evergreen Lanes in the Mustang. "I thought we were going to shoot pool at Ernie's."

"We can do that later," Tom said.

Buck wasn't easily put off. "I thought you didn't like bowling because Dirk wipes the floor with you."

Dirk might wipe the floor with him in bowling, but Tom could wipe the basketball court with Dirk. So they were even steven on that score.

"I just want to check something out, then we can leave," Tom said, trying to explain as little as possible.

Lights from the huge Bowl-O-Rama sign made the interior of the muscle car as bright as daylight when Tom drove past it to the crowded parking area.

"Looks like the place to be." Buck whistled. "Who knew bowling had made such a comeback?"

The parking lot was far more crowded than Tom expected. He was still edgy from the lights-out incident the night before, and he was worried about Jude. She was sweet and naïve, and Dirk was sure to take advantage of her.

Not because Dirk intended to sleep with Jude, but because he was trying to make Tom jealous enough to claim Jude for himself, leaving Dirk to win the money. His former roommate was using her to gain an upper hand in the wager.

And if Tom wasn't careful, Dirk's ploy could work. For the past twenty-four hours, Tom had been unable to think of anything but Jude.

Heck, if they hadn't been at his aunt and uncle's house last night, there was no telling where things might have led.

"I'll put our names down for a lane," Buck offered.

"Thanks," Tom said. "I'll order a pitcher of beer."

He hadn't been to Evergreen Lanes in a while, but he knew it was a favorite haunt of Dirk's. The layout was typical: a raised level behind the lanes with booths where people could eat, drink, and watch the bowlers, and rows of seats on the lower level by the electronic scorekeepers.

His pulse pounded in his throat and Tom blamed it on the noisy impact of balls on pins.

He checked out lane after lane, beginning to think he was wasting his time and that Dirk hadn't brought Jude to his favorite bowling alley and he'd taken her somewhere else instead.

And then he saw them.

The second lane on the far end.

Jude was wearing a short, flared skirt and a soft-pink sweater—didn't she know it was freezing cold outside—and even in clunky red-and-blue bowling shoes, her legs looked spectacular.

Dirk stood directly behind her, one arm wrapped around her waist, the other showing her how to guide the ball down the lane.

Jealousy bit a big green chunk out of Tom, and he had a sudden urge to storm up to Dirk and punch him squarely in the nose. Instead, he ground his teeth.

"We have a half hour wait," Buck said, catching up with Tom.

"Uh-huh." Tom headed down to the area behind the bowlers and Buck followed.

"Where are we going?"

Tom scarcely heard what his friend was saying; he was too busy thinking of what he had to say to Jude. She might not be pleased to see him—especially after last night.

And Dirk? How would he react?

Who cared? Tom was here to see Jude and tell her the truth about why Dirk asked her out. Let him recover from that.

"Hey," Buck said. "Isn't that your friend Dirk?"

"It is."

Buck whistled under his breath. "Who's the hot brunette?"

Tom didn't bother to answer. He took a seat directly behind the lane Dirk and Jude were in and pressed the call button to order a pitcher of beer. Buck settled beside him, pulled out his cell phone, and started leafing through social media.

Dirk turned and caught sight of him, and a look of sheer triumphant crossed his smug mug. Coming here had been a tactical mistake and it gave Dirk the upper hand. His buddy knew Tom was interested in Jude and he was using it to his benefit.

And as for Jude? She was bound to label him a jealous jerk, which in retrospect, he was. Chastising himself for letting his emotions get the better of him, Tom turned to tell Buck they were leaving.

But before he could get the words out of his mouth, sly Dirk winked and move to slip his arm around Jude's waist as she stood to take her turn. Leaning in close, Dirk whispered something in her ear.

What was he saying?

Tom's pulse quickened and his mouth went instantly dry. *Do not rise to the bait; do not rise to the bait.*

Grinding his teeth, Tom jumped to his feet, and feigning surprise, said, "Why, hello, Poomph," he said. "Fancy meeting you here."

11

"You've got this," Dirk whispered as he slid his arm around her waist.

Or course she had it. Jude had bowled in a league for three years. Annoyed, she moved away from him.

She was picking up her bowling ball when she heard the sound of Tom's voice. Jerking at the sound, she bounced the ball back on the rack where it narrowly missed falling off onto her foot.

"You okay?" asked Dirk, who was still hovering.

With a stiff nod, Jude picked up the ball again, did *not* look around for Tom, stepped up to the line for her turn, and rolled a perfect gutter ball.

Embarrassed, Jude spun around to see Tom sitting behind a tall older man, grinning at her like he'd come here to rattle her on purpose and ruin her date.

Damn it. Dirk—and the things he'd told her about Tom on the way to the bowling alley—was right.

Tom Brunswick had a competitive streak a mile wide and he'd come here to vie for her attention while she was on a date with his friend.

Oh, dude! Not cool. He was taking competition to a whole new level, and she didn't appreciate being used as a chess piece in Tom and Dirk's silly games.

"Don't feel bad about the gutter ball," Dirk reassured her. "Happens to the best of us."

It didn't happen to Jude. She was a good bowler, but now Tom had caused her to look foolish in front of her date and she was irritated.

"He followed us," Jude muttered, glowering at Tom. "I can't believe it."

"Told you so." Dirk smirked.

Tom caught her eye and waved wildly.

"You told him where we were going?" Dirk asked.

"He was with me when you phoned me yesterday and overheard our conversation."

"But you see what I mean, right? He can't let anything go."

"Just ignore him." She turned her back on Tom, steamed that he'd shown up to meddle in her date, and she finished her turn. The second ball was a split that left two pins standing.

What the devil was he doing, trailing her on her date with Dirk? Did it have anything to do with what happened last night? Had the kiss meant as much to him as it had her? His presence here seemed to suggest it and hope lifted her up far higher than was prudent, but she couldn't seem to help herself. She'd lain awake far into the night, thinking about his mind-bending kiss.

"Much as I would like to ignore him," Dirk said. "He's making himself comfortable in our seating area."

Jude groaned. "Fine. I'll deal with him."

Dirk looked amused and made a sweeping gesture with his arm that said go for it.

"No." Jude shook her head. "I've changed my mind. I'm not playing into whatever scheme he's got up his sleeve." She gave Dirk the most charming smile she could muster. "It's your turn."

"You sure you don't want to go talk to him?"

"Absolutely."

"It's all right if you do."

"I don't."

"Okay. Your call." Dirk chuckled and picked up his ball.

But despite her declarations to the contrary, as Dirk sized up his shot, Jude couldn't stop herself from striding over to where Tom sat spread out,

LORI WILDE & & PAM ANDREWS HANSON

taking up more than his allotment of space on the bench.

"What are you doing here?" she demanded.

That aw-shucks, lopsided grin crossed his face.

"You're here to mess with Dirk, aren't you?" she accused. "Throw him off his game. Embarrass him."

"Not at all," Tom said with a devastating smile. "I came to tell you something important."

Ooh, that took her breath away, but she didn't want him to know how much he could affect her. "While I'm on my *date?*"

"Jude, there's something you must know about—"

"We've already covered this last night." She snorted and curled her hands on her hips. "You've already warned me. Dirk's a player. I know. I don't care. I'm not going to let you sabotage my evening. You've got to get over this ridiculous jealousy. It's not a good look."

"That's not why I'm here."

"No?"

"This is about me." He gulped visibly. "About you. About us."

"Us?"

Dirk came up to stand behind Jude and put a hand at her waist.

She didn't like that and gave him a "step-off" stare.

Looking sheepish, Dirk dropped his hand and backed up.

Well, will you look at that? She was making her wishes known. Raising her chin a little higher, Jude turned back to Tom and caught him shooting Dirk a gloaty smile. Exasperated, she snapped her fingers in front of his face.

"You," she said. "May I speak to you in private?" To Dirk, she said, "I'll just be a sec."

"Hurry back. It's boring without you." Dirk waved and didn't look at all perturbed. She wasn't quite sure what to make of this whole thing.

They left the lane area, and Jude marched to an alcove near the restrooms and waited for Tom to join her. She felt amped up, as if a low-level hum of electricity were running through her entire body, but she had no idea why.

Beyond Tom's unique scent jumbling up her mind.

"Look," he said, raising his hands and then pushing his palms downward simultaneously. "Please let me explain before you go off on me."

She prided herself on being a rational person who was willing to give anyone the benefit of the doubt. Jude folded her arms across her chest, tilted her head, and said, "I'm listening."

He seemed surprised by that. Inhaling deeply, he exhaled the breath in a rush. "See, there's this bet..."

"A bet? What kind of bet?"

Tom winced. "There were four of us initially. Frat brothers from college. Dirk and I are the last two left."

"Left?"

"In the competition."

"What kind of competition?" she repeated, stringing Tom along.

On the way to the bowling alley after their dinner, Dirk had told Jude about the bet and the real reason he'd asked her out, but Tom didn't need to know what she knew. Let him sweat it out.

Ooh, that wasn't something a "nice" woman would say. Take that, Jaxon!

"A no-sex bet," Tom mumbled.

Enjoying his embarrassment maybe a little too much, Jude cupped a palm around her ear. "I'm sorry, it's so noisy in here. What did you say?"

Meeting her gaze, he said a bit louder, "A no-sex bet."

"What's that?" Jude asked, pretending to be clue-less. It was fun watching him squirm.

"Ever seen the movie *40 Days and 40 Nights*?"

"I might have heard about it. An old flick with Josh Hartnett not having sex for forty days and forty nights."

"Actually, our bet is really more along the lines of a *Seinfeld* episode. 'The Contest.'"

"Really?" She struggled not to laugh. She wanted him to think she was put off by such immature behavior. "You're competing to be the master of your domain?"

"Yes, well, except with our bet, it's no sex of any kind." Tom cleared his throat and had the good grace to look embarrassed. "That's why Dirk asked you out. He's just trying to get me jealous, so I'll want you all the more, and he's hoping we'll get together and I'll be out of the contest, leaving him to walk away with twelve hundred dollars."

"Oh, really?" Now she *was* a bit irked. "Let me unpack this. You're saying that in order to get turned on, you have to have someone else chasing after the woman you're interested in?"

"No!" He snorted, a little too fast and a little loud, his cheeks flushing red.

"Are you sure?"

"Dirk has nothing to do with how much you turn me on." His voice turned husky.

"I'm beginning to think your mom and aunts are right and your competitive streak is a sickness."

"It's not like that." He sounded almost desperate now, as if he realized far too late what a miscalculation he'd made.

"Then why are you here? We're merely acquaintances who shared a kiss last night. We have no claims on each other." This was the same thing she'd been telling herself all day. "Why did you feel compelled to follow me on my date and confess about the bet? You could have just stayed away and kept your mouth shut. Or if you had to tell me, you could have waited until our date tomorrow."

"Are you still going out with me tomorrow?" he asked.

In that moment, he looked so freaking vulnerable, it was all she could do to hold on to her pique. "That all depends on you."

Tom hung his head and glanced down. "Your shoe is untied."

"What?" Jude asked, trying to puzzle out what was truly going on. Dirk had told her one thing, Tom another.

Without answering, Tom sank to his knees in front of her.

"What are you doing?" Confused, she blinked down at the loose flapping laces of her bowling shoes.

The man was tying her shoes!

It was a simple act, but it felt far too intimate. The considerate gesture placed him firmly at her feet, almost as if he were groveling. She felt, in the moment, like a revered goddess. It was a heady feeling and a deep yearning swept through her.

A yearning that, quite frankly, scared the dickens out of her.

The pulse at her throat ticked and her chest tightened.

Tom's tousled dark hair was so close she had to squeeze her fingers into fists to keep from checking its silky softness. He was the kind of man who could make a woman completely lose her head, and suddenly all she could think about was getting naked with him. Their kiss last night seemed chaste compared to the images dancing through her head.

But he'd taken a celibacy vow, and now she had a challenge of her own going with Dirk. Her game? Teach Tom an important lesson about being overly competitive. A little competition was fine. Too much brought out an unflattering side. The win-at-all-costs attitude was dangerous.

So why did she suddenly want desperately to win her side bet with Dirk?

"There." He patted her foot and stood up. "All tied up."

"Thank you," she rasped. Her voice sounded different even to her own ears. He had to have heard the strange sultry quality too. "For tying my shoes."

They were eye to eye.

Her head spun, and her body filled with a river of hot, rippling tingles.

"Jude," he murmured at the same time she whispered, "Tom."

The bowling alley ceased to exist. The noises faded and the people disappeared, and it was just the two of them in their own private cocoon.

He leaned in.

She went up on the balls of her feet in her freshly tied bowling shoes.

Sweeping her into his arms, his lips came down on hers.

In bowling parlance, his kiss would have been a strike that scattered the pins into the next lane. He kissed her full on the mouth, his tongue parting her lips, the intensity of it vibrating all the way to her toes.

Last night was nothing compared to this kiss and she wanted to melt against him and savor this moment forever. She was breathless, wanting more, and she hadn't even had a chance to kiss him back.

"Have a good night." His words caressed her ears; she'd never heard a voice so compellingly sensual.

She reached out, weak with longing and needing something more from him to cushion their separation.

But he'd already pulled back. "See you tomorrow

night for our date. I hope you've picked something adventuresome."

Oh, wow, no. Not yet.

"Wait," she said.

He paused, his eyes shiny. "Yes?"

"How about we turn the tables on Dirk?" she dared, plunging into the plan that Dirk had outlined on the way over to Evergreen Lanes.

It felt like a double cross and the nice woman inside her balked. But the entire point was to shed her Goody Two-Shoes image and fully *live* for the first time in her life and that's what she wanted.

To prove Jaxon was wrong about her. That she wasn't boring.

One of Tom's eyebrows jumped up higher on his forehead. "What do you have in mind?"

"Let me get this straight. You're saying that Dirk thinks by dating me, it will make you jealous and your jealousy will make you want to stake your claim on me. Am I understanding this correctly?"

"He's used the ploy before."

"And by staking your claim, it will lead to you giving up on the bet so you can get with me."

"That's about the size of it."

"Hmm."

His eyes flared with dark intensity. "What are you thinking?"

LORI WILDE & & PAM ANDREWS HANSON

"Here's an idea." Jude paused, knowing she was headed down a slippery slope and hoping she was wily enough to pull off this double cross.

Tom stepped closer. There was a sheen of perspiration on his forehead, and it was all she could do not to reach over and dab it off.

"What if," she proposed, offering the solution Dirk had fed her on the drive over. "I act super interested in Dirk and get him charged up enough to lose the bet? In other words, the puppet master gets played."

Tom stroked his chin and he looked pensive. "It's an interesting idea, but I don't want you to compromise your own values for our stupid rivalry."

"You let me worry about me."

"Are you interested in Dirk?"

Jude studied him. She'd never seen a face quite like his. All his features were ordinary enough—maybe "regular" was more descriptive—but combined they added up to much more than an attractive guy. She'd love to be a sculptor and use him as her model. She could almost feel his masculine beauty taking form in wet clay under her fingers.

C'mon. She was kidding herself. What she really wanted was to stroke his cheek, feel the whisper of his breath on her fingertips, press her lips against his lids—

She was incredibly attracted to him. She couldn't deny the truth any longer, and because of that, she needed to be careful in how she responded. She could blow the whole thing with the wrong words.

"No. I mean he's great-looking and charming, but you're right, he's a player, and while I am looking for fun, I eventually want more."

That didn't calm Tom at all. He shook his head and his brown eyes widened in alarm. "Does this mean you're actually considering going home with Dirk?"

She heard the panic in his voice and suppressed a smile. This was going to work. "Don't you want to win that bet?"

"No, no!" He shook his head so vigorously she feared it would swivel right off his body. "Not this way. I don't want you to sleep with him! Please, don't sleep with him."

"Tom," she said in all seriousness, a bit giddy with her own power, "I'm a nice woman."

"But you're working hard to change that." Seriously, Tom looked positively panic-stricken.

"Not all in one night." She winked. "Your bet does preclude *any* sexual activity, right? So self-indulgences are grounds for...er...shall we say, discharge from the contest."

He didn't comment on her pun, but he shifted his

weight from leg to leg, back and forth in an aggressive sway as if torn between wanting to beat Dirk in the competition and keeping Jude as far away as possible from his horndog buddy.

"Are you saying that you plan to get Dirk charged up enough so that he'll go home and..." Tom's entire body tensed.

Jude was feeling decidedly naughty and she couldn't stop a wicked grin from overtaking her face. She'd set the bait and Tom had taken it. He was hooked.

"Lose the bet without me," she said, finishing the sentence for him.

❧ 12 ❧

Last night, watching Jude flirt like crazy with Dirk had just about killed him. As part of Jude's plan to goose Dirk into losing the bet, she'd invited Tom and Buck to bowl with them, and then she'd proceeded to hang all over Dirk, putting her plan into action.

He hated every second of it and only the thought of Dirk losing the bet kept him from begging Jude to go home with him instead. Dirk did need to be taught a lesson, but Tom wasn't convinced this was the way to do it.

It ended up being the most miserable two hours of his life.

To his surprise, Dirk had been enthusiastic about Tom and Buck joining them, which raised Tom's suspicions as to what his buddy had up his sleeve. He didn't trust Dirk any farther than he could pick him up and thrust him face-first down the bowling lane.

By the end of the evening, he was flat-out sulking and the only thing that boosted his spirits was the thought of winning that bet.

Afterward, as he lay in bed thinking of Jude in that cute outfit, his body hardened and the temptation to drop out of the contest was overwhelming. She filled his head—the sight of her shapely body, the smell of her intoxicating fragrance, the sound of her soft, beguiling voice.

But that was what Dirk wanted him to do, and Tom would be damned if he'd give his buddy the upper hand.

All the next day, he waited for Dirk to text him and tell him he was out of the bet, but Dirk did not. So much for Jude's plan, apparently. Dirk had a cast-iron constitution.

Yeah, well, so do you.

Unless Dirk was dishonest.

His buddy could be manipulative, and he lived to gamble and take risks, but Tom had never known Dirk to tell an outright lie.

So either Dirk was still the "master of his domain" or...

A startling new—and frankly terrifying—thought seized him. What if Dirk really liked Jude? What if he wanted her for himself? What if Tom was wrong and Dirk wasn't just using Jude to get him to drop out of the competition?

Those questions plagued him all day long, and it was with great relief when he pulled up to Jude's apartment complex at six thirty that Saturday evening. Tonight, she'd be with him and not Dirk.

Suck on that, Poomph.

Jude met him at the door, looking like a total knockout in a navy-blue dress and scarlet stilettos. She looked so stunning, he feared he was under-dressed in slacks and a sports jacket.

"You look like a million bucks," he said, stupefied. She'd held nothing back. Her soft dark hair fell in big curls around her shoulders and she smelled like heaven.

"Thank you." Her eyes filled with appreciation for his comment.

"Jaxon is a total fool."

Her smiled broadened. "Thank you for validating me."

"I'm not trying to validate you," he said. "I mean what I say. You're ravishing."

"Flattery will get you everywhere." She winked as

she pulled the door to her apartment closed and locked it behind them.

Okay, he needed to nip that conversation in the bud before he got really charged up. "Where are we going?"

"I'll give you directions when we're in the car."

"Ahh, mysterious."

"I want to keep you interested."

"Oh..." He eyed her up and down. "You have nothing to worry about on that score. I am beyond interested."

"How's the bet going?" she asked as they went down the three staircases together. "Is Dirk still in the competition after last night?"

"Yes."

"Aww, I'm sorry I failed to get you the results you wanted."

"Don't be. I don't even want to think about Dirk. Tonight is all about you and me."

"Hmm," she mused as if he hadn't said a word. "I guess I'm not as charming as I thought I was. I'll make another date with him and see if I can turn up the heat."

"No!" Tom exclaimed so loudly his voice echoed in the confines of the stairwell.

"Don't you want to win?"

"Not like this," he said.

"Oh, really? That doesn't sound like the Tom Brunswick I've come to know."

"Yeah, well, some things are more important than winning." He surprised the heck out of himself with that statement.

"Since when?" She laughed lightly.

Since she'd been rubbing up against Dirk all night at the bowling alley. Tom ground his teeth, remembering as they hit the first-floor landing and stepped out into the cold November night air.

He inhaled a bracing lungful of chilled oxygen and it helped to clear his head...until he took Jude's arm to guide her down the sidewalk dusted with snow and a fresh assault of longing blasted through him. Why *was* he clinging to a decade worth of rivalry when he could let go and explore this chemistry with Jude? All he had to do was call Dirk and tell him he was out of the contest.

Easy-peasy.

Why was it so hard?

Once they were in the Mustang, Jude gave him directions to where they were going, and he recognized it as a hip new nightclub on the other side of town that Dirk frequented. It had, in fact, been the club where the four former frat boys had made their bet.

Jude's choice of venues surprised him.

"Are you sure you want to go to The Loophole?" he asked.

"Sure, why not?" She said it almost too easily, as if her decision had been a calculated one but she didn't want him to know it.

Or maybe he was reading things into her voice that weren't there. Sometimes, his competitiveness made him a little paranoid, particularly in relationship to Dirk.

"The Loophole doesn't seem like your kind of place."

"All the more reason to go. My 'usual' kind of place is nice and boring. Like Rocky's. I'm ready to kick up my heels for real. You game to kick them with me?"

"I like Rocky's," he said, feeling a little defensive and not knowing why.

"Me too, but it's the kind of place families hang out at. The Loophole is not." She had a point. The Loophole was the antithesis to a family-friendly establishment.

"Have you ever been there?" he asked.

"No, but Dirk told me about it last night."

That explained that.

Jude bebopped in her seat. "I can't wait to boogie down with you."

Twenty minutes later, feeling decidedly uneasy and braced for a wild night, Tom escorted her into the club.

TOM WAS RIGHT BUT JUDE WASN'T ABOUT TO admit it.

The Loophole was *not* her kind of place.

For one thing, it was so noisy on a Saturday night that conversation was nearly impossible. The funky DJ relentlessly blasted out tunes with suggestive lyrics and hard, driving beats. For another thing, sardines in a can were packed more loosely than people in the club. With this many people, there had to be some kind of fire code violation. People who, for the most part, were very scantily dressed for November.

She wished she could be more like those blithe souls who could express themselves so freely and not care about public opinion. Tom was right on that score too. She didn't need to learn how to be wild— although teasing Tom last night by feigning interest in Dirk had been rather fun, especially since Dirk was in on the joke. She needed to learn how to stop caring what other people thought of her.

And that included Tom Brunswick.

By some miracle, he'd managed to find them a minuscule bistro table in a far corner. It was sticky with the drinks from the last occupants, but at least they didn't have to stand in the madding crowd.

Jude took a deep breath and tried to settle down, but her stomach was in her throat. In theory, she wanted to cut loose, have fun, dance until closing time, and then take Tom back to her place and conspire for him to lose that bet.

Or at least that was the plan.

Eyeballing Tom from her peripheral vision, she'd never seen him looking more handsome. He was wearing a gray herringbone sport coat over dark-gray pleated trousers and a black knit shirt. He'd gotten a haircut, not short but stylish, and fragrant aftershave wafted around his freshly shaved face.

"Here, let me fix this," she murmured and leaned in closer, playing the bold woman to the hilt. She reached up and adjusted the fold in his collar, letting her fingers graze the underside of his chin and linger lightly.

He made a low, barely perceptible grunt.

"There." She smiled a bit smugly, patting his neck the way he'd patted her foot the night before. "Much better."

He turned his shoulders away from her and scanned the crowd.

Sucking in a deep breath, she wondered if she'd overplayed her strategy.

Feeling a little insecure, Jude made a production of crossing her legs. She knew her ankles looked great in the red stilettos and hoped to snag his attention.

Tom waved to someone across the room. Apparently, he came here often enough to meet people. But of course, he was a man who liked bold women and this place was packed to the rafters with them.

Desperate to get some reaction from him, she found his leg under the table and rubbed her calf against his. If this didn't thaw him... She slipped one shoe off and let her toe crawl up his leg.

"Here's comes our waiter," he said, pointing at someone carrying a tray surfing through the wave of undulating bodies.

And he *moved* his leg away.

Well, that was a slap in the face. She was practically throwing herself at him and he wasn't reacting.

He wants to win that bet.

Hmm. This plan was going to be harder than she thought. Tom's mother and aunts were right. His competitive streak ran just a little too deep. If she didn't know the reason why he was resisting her, she might get a complex. While she wasn't a bold woman by nature, she had enough healthy self-esteem to know when a man was attracted to her.

Tom was attracted.

Unless there was another reason that he'd just taken off his sports jacket and draped it over his lap.

Grinning, she upped the ante.

It was dark and they were in a secluded corner—as secluded as one could get in a sardine tin—and his sports jacket provided sufficient coverage for what she had in mind.

Daringly, Jude turned saucy. She kicked off her heels, freed her bare toes, and leaned forward.

Tom might love to win, but tonight, so did she.

Mustering all her courage, Jude lifted one leg and let her toes come to rest squarely on her target.

***

TOM WAS SHOCKED!

And more.

Much more.

Her busy little toes burrowed against his zipper, causing more havoc than she could imagine. Oh no, no, no. He couldn't have this. Not here. Not now. Not when his body ached for her. Craved her.

In self-defense, he caught her foot and moved it away fast.

"I'm getting a whiskey sour. What are you having?" It was probably the dumbest thing he'd ever said. At least, it felt that way under the circumstances.

He blamed himself. He was the one who'd told her not to care what other people thought of her.

Truth?

He hadn't expected her to *do* it. You could just tell she was a people pleaser from way back, but now it seemed she was taking the old Ricky Nelson tune "Garden Party" to heart and was pleasing herself.

Which given a different time, different place, different conditions, he'd applaud her audacity.

But here, now, with the bet hanging over his head, Tom wasn't at all sure how he felt about her toes in his lap. He'd thought he'd love it when she finally let herself fully be who she was.

Instead, he was...*scared*.

He was witnessing a shy introvert stepping fully into her sexual power and it made him so damn hard he could barely stand himself.

"Ginger ale," Jude said.

He was so wrapped up in staring at her sexy lips that Tom had already forgotten the question he'd asked her. "Huh?"

"You do know ginger ale is the same price as alcoholic drinks, right?" the waiter asked Jude as he leaned over to put napkins on the sticky tabletop.

"Really?" Jude gave him a look that said *pfft*. "Why?"

The waiter shrugged. "Don't ask me. I just work here."

She frowned. "I don't appreciate being pressured into drinking."

"Lady, I don't know what the problem is," the waiter snapped. "Drink. Don't drink. I don't care. I was just trying to tell you that it costs the same to drink as it does not to."

"Oh my goodness." Jude brought both hands to her mouth. Even in the darkness, Tom could see her blush. "I'm so sorry. I was playing at being bold and it came out bitchy. That's not the way I intended it. Please forgive me."

"*Gurrl.*" The waiter waved an expressive hand. "Don't worry about it. You're a little ray of sunshine compared to a lot of our customers. That's why *I* was so touchy. I just got bawled out by some lady who ordered the wrong drink but insisted I was in the wrong."

"Not fair."

"C'est la vie. So, just the ginger ale, hon?"

"Just the ginger ale." Jude nodded and the waiter moved on.

Tom noticed she slipped a ten-dollar bill from her purse and left it on the table as a tip. He added a twenty and ten to cover the cost of their drinks. The Loophole wasn't cheap.

Watching her navigate the terrain between nice and brazen was like watching a newborn baby deer trying to walk for the first time—all spindly legged and uncertain. He turned his head to hide his smile. He doubted that she would appreciate being compared to a fawn, and he didn't want her to think he was laughing at her.

They people-watched for a few minutes, and then the DJ played a new hit song.

"Would you like to dance?" he shouted over the music.

She shook her head. "It's too crowded."

The waiter brought their drinks, saw the money, and pounced on it. "Thank you so much! You're a doll! But don't you want to run a tab?" He shifted his gaze to Tom when he asked his.

"This'll do for now," Tom said.

"Okay, I'll circle back in a bit to check on you." The waiter departed for the second time.

Tom didn't know what to do. She thought it was too crowded to dance and she wasn't drinking.

He ached for an excuse to hold her in his arms again, but the nightclub's style of music was a far cry from the waltzable slow dances Tara had selected for her wedding reception.

"You sure you don't want to dance?" he asked.

She shook her head and hugged herself as if she were cold, but with so many bodies crammed into the space, it was overly warm in here.

He studied her for a long moment. Earnest face, big blue eyes, that fall of soft brown hair curling to her shoulders. Her smile was genuine, but beneath it, he could tell she was uncomfortable. The Loophole was not her kind of place.

"There's a game room in the back," he hollered above the music. "Pool, shuffleboard, darts, foosball."

"I'm not very good at those games but if you'd like, I can give it a shot." She bobbed her head.

"You're not having a good time," he said.

"I am," she enthused, clearly trying too hard. "This is interesting. I don't go to many places like this."

"It's hot and it's loud and the drinks are far too expensive."

"Granted," she said. "But it's good to step out of my comfort zone once in a while."

"Can I ask you a serious question?"

She pursed her lips and looked a bit worried. "Mmm."

"Why did you suggest we come here?" He took a drink of his whiskey sour and found it watered down.

She lifted her shoulders and the corners of her mouth simultaneously. "Dirk told me you loved this place."

"Not true. *Dirk* loves this place," Tom corrected, irritated at the mention of his friend. "I come here because this is where he likes to hang out."

"So you're not a fan of The Loophole?"

Tom shrugged. "I can take it or leave it."

"Oh. I didn't know that."

His eyes met hers. "Would you like to get out of here?"

"Yes, please." Her smile was a reward and it lit him up in unexpected places.

"Before we go, I have another question to ask you."

"Okay." She cocked her head, studying him so intently he started to wonder if he had something on his face.

Feeling self-conscious, he ran a palm over his mouth. "Tell me how *you* would like to spend the rest of evening and be completely honest. Stop worrying about pleasing me."

Jude cringed. "If I tell you the truth, you'll think I'm the most boring person on the planet."

"Try me," he said, irked that he had to shout the

conversation. "What would you normally be doing on a Saturday night?"

"Catching a movie at the Tavern Cinema."

"Sounds perfect. C'mon. Grab your coat and let's blow this popsicle stand."

This time, Jude's real smile was as glittery as unicorn rainbows.

Sitting in the darkened theatre, waiting for the show to start, Tom could smell Jude's sweet scent mingling with the aroma of buttery popcorn and spicy jalapeños. They'd ordered the extra-large bucket to share along with fully loaded nachos and beer.

He tried not to think about how much he wanted to kiss her or how soft her hand was on the armrest between them. He had a bet to win and these kinds of thoughts didn't serve his goal. Not in the least.

And then, as the movie started, Jude leaned over to rest her head on his shoulder, and Tom just about unraveled.

He was getting in too deep and he feared he would end up hurting her.

Is that what you're afraid of? challenged a snarky

voice at the back of his brain. *Or are you afraid of getting hurt yourself?*

There was a reason he kept his romantic entanglements light. He was terrified of getting his heart broken. Throwing himself into crafting furniture, telling himself that starting his business and getting it on solid ground was the reason why he couldn't afford to get serious about anyone.

The real truth was that he'd been hiding from the kinds of feelings Jude stirred in him. It was why he dated women who weren't interested in anything long term. Even though Jude had sworn that all she wanted was to have fun, he didn't buy it.

She was a happily-ever-after kind of woman, and the man who ended up with her would be lucky beyond his wildest dreams.

Jude was the total package—smart, funny, gorgeous, and she didn't mind his daffy family. In fact, she even seemed to like them, and they liked her. Several times this week his mother had texted him to ask when he was bringing Jude around again.

All he had to do was stay safely out of her way until the bet was over and yet, he couldn't seem to resist temptation. He could have called off the date. He should have called off the date, but he hadn't.

Why not?

What was he doing with her? He wasn't sure

himself. He should either stop seeing her or go for a long swim in cold water, but he wasn't ready to jump into Lake Michigan—or stop seeing her.

He wasn't ready to push her out of his life, but he didn't know where to go from here.

Sure, he could forfeit the bet and take her to bed the way his body was begging him to do. The way her inviting smile, and the feel of her head on his shoulder, were encouraging him to do.

Surprisingly, despite the sexual tension, the rest of the evening was a blast. For Tom at least. The movie was hilarious and unexpectedly poignant as the main character learned to face his fears and embrace life— which in the end, included finding true love.

The character's growth arc felt far too familiar, and he found himself wondering if Jude had picked the movie on purpose as some kind of message, but no, she seemed completely guileless, and the flick was so good, he vowed to stop overthinking things.

Just a coincidence.

And when the happily ever after came with closing credits, and Jude reached for his hand, Tom couldn't resist gently squeezing her soft little hand as his confounded heart swelled inside his chest.

Afterward, they went out for frozen yogurt and when she added gummy bears to her pink lemonade froyo, he burst out in a big grin. She considered herself boring, but she looked at the world through such open and wondrous eyes he couldn't help being charmed.

They sat in a back booth and over their desserts talked about themselves, not his bet, not her ex-fiancé, not Dirk. He told her how he'd started the store, and she filled him in about graduate school. They discovered they both loved hiking and camping. Tom confessed he could make a mean omelet, but was otherwise pretty hopeless in the kitchen. Jude revealed her father had taught her to change the oil in her car, but she always managed to persuade someone else to do it for her.

Then she blinked rapidly at him.

"All right, all right." He laughed and raised his palms. "I'll change the oil in your car."

"You don't have to." She grinned. "I went electric."

"Lucky me." He chuckled. "Look how you wrapped me around your little finger."

"Did I do that?"

"Don't act like you don't know I'm putty in your hands."

"Not hardly."

"Oh, very hardly."

She cast a surreptitious glance at his zipper and

Tom denounced all her claims that she wasn't a wild woman. She was red hot.

Outside the yogurt store, the evening was overcast but mild with little wind; it boded well for a milder winter. When he walked her to the outer door of her complex, it was nearly midnight.

"Can I come up?" he asked, following her into the vestibule, even as he knew it was a risky thing to do.

"Sorry, not on our first date."

"This isn't our first date."

"Yes, it is."

"Our first date was Tara's wedding."

"Doesn't count."

"Why not?"

"You needed a warm body for a date. I was handy, and you felt sorry for me because I got stood up at the altar. I'm not letting a pity date be our first."

"What about Aunt Pru's birthday party?"

"I'm not sure what that was all about, but it wasn't a date. I didn't even have time to change. I smelled like eight hours in the library."

"A very nice scent I might add." He leaned in closer.

"And last night certainly wasn't a date."

"Of course not, you were with Dirk."

"You tied my shoelaces and then kissed me."

"I did," he confirmed.

"I can't help wondering something though."

"What's that?" He was so close he could feel the warmth of her pink lemonade breath on his cheek.

She was having fun with him, and that was more erotic than her toes caressing his crotch at The Loophole.

"Would you have kissed me if I hadn't been with Dirk?"

Considering that he wouldn't have been at the bowling alley at all if she hadn't been there with Dirk, he couldn't say yes.

"Dirk isn't here right now," he said.

"Isn't he?" she asked, edging away from him. "In your head? Aren't you dithering about whether you should indeed come up if I gave you the green light because you want so badly to best your buddy?"

"No," he said, but his tone had no tooth to it. "I want to be with you. It's as simple as that."

"Enough to blow off your bet?"

"I do."

She swung her gaze into his like she was swinging a bat, and Tom literally jumped at the force of her stare. "Do you?"

"Y-yes."

"That doesn't sound very convincing."

"I want to come up." Being turned down always challenged him, but this was different. He wanted to be with her for a while longer on any terms, even though he knew nothing was going to happen between them tonight.

"No, I don't think so," she said and nodded.

Mixed messages. He got it. He was filled with contradictions too.

"Can I kiss you good night?" The devil made him ask—or maybe it was because he could still remember the feel of her foot burrowing against him.

"Maybe a little peck on the cheek," she said, pointing.

He was playing with fire, but it was hard to think rationally when she was driving him crazy. He wanted her in his arms, in his bed...

And in his life.

Whoa! Slow way down, Brunswick.

Rashness poured him like water through a wide-open drain. He bent his head and gently let his lips tease the corner of her mouth, nibbling a little as he eased his arms around her. Her coat was open, and her breasts pressed against him, firm and delectable under the soft material.

He was stunned by his own reaction; he hadn't even kissed her properly, and he was already harder than flint. He tried to blame it on his celibate lifestyle of late, but he knew it was Jude.

All Jude.

She raised her arm and circled his neck, her gloved fingers stroking the skin under his collar.

He couldn't take any more. He kissed her hard and long, parting her lips with his tongue and forcefully taking what he wanted, holding her head in his hands and not sparing himself or her.

This was no first-date kiss; he was going too far, too fast, so eager for the sweetness of her mouth, he forgot himself. Using all the self-control he possessed, he backed off, giving her a chance to protest or leave.

Instead, she tugged his head down, pressing her pelvis against him, weakening all his resolve in the sheer torturous pleasure of holding her close. He slid her coat off her shoulders and ran his hands down her back, gripping her buttocks, squeezing and urging her even closer until he was almost lifting her off the floor.

The tiny vestibule was steamy warm, and he heard her gasping for air even as his own lungs panted for oxygen. He didn't know how they'd come so far so fast. It was a fantasy come to life—Jude locked against him, riding his knee between her thighs as he tried to clear his head and still not lose what was happening.

"Maybe you *could* come up for a few minutes," she said in a husky whisper.

This time, he did scoop her into his arms, and she

let out a whoop as he carried her up the first flight of stairs.

"Put me down, you loon." She laughed, but he could tell she was enjoying herself.

He slowed on the second staircase but kept going.

"Tom," she said. "This is silly. Please put me down."

"Almost there." He panted, sweat popping out on his forehead.

"Tom!"

"Did I ever tell you I tried out to be a fireman?"

"I can see where you get your stamina. Why didn't you become a fireman?"

"I did," he said. "And then I realized I was trying to live someone else's dream for me."

"Who's?" she asked as he set her on the ground in front of her apartment.

"Amanda's."

"Your first real girlfriend."

Tom nodded. "Amanda thought making furniture was too sedate."

"Just like Jaxon thought I was boring," Jude mused.

"That's how I know you have to be true to yourself and let other people sort themselves out. You can't twist yourself into a pretzel trying to be something you're not. I tried it for Amanda. It didn't work."

"Do you mean like being so obsessively competitive that you lose sight of your real motive in service to the goal?"

"Wait, what?"

"Why did you accept Dirk's bet in the first place?" she asked.

Her question caught him off guard and he stood blinking at her, still trying to fully catch his breath.

"Why are you sticking to it?" she went on. "There's nothing holding you to the bet other than this fierce rivalry."

The question deserved an answer, but it wasn't as clear cut as she made it sound.

"The rivalry might have been fun when you were young, but isn't it time to let that stuff go?"

"I've always had a competitive streak," he said, feeling a little defensive, but only because her questions were making him uncomfortable. "I'm a twin. Competition comes with the territory."

For the first time, he fully understood that his relentless drive to be the best had consequences. He'd thought winning was a good thing. His determined mindset had gotten him where he was in his chosen field. Made him a great furniture maker. It kept him in tip-top physical shape, but...

It had cost him too.

The biggest casualty?

Intimacy.

In a competition, you couldn't afford to be truly intimate with someone. Intimacy gave away your vulnerabilities and left you wide open for assault by your enemies.

Something dawned on him then. Something that had been lurking in the back of his mind since he'd met Jude. He'd been going about relationships as if they were competitions. Keeping score between who was up and who was down. He did it with his sister; he did it with his friends, and he'd done it with the women he dated.

Now, with Jude, he wanted to break that pattern.

"One more question," she said. "If that's okay. What happens if neither you nor Dirk caves? What if you both make it to the forty-day deadline? Who wins?"

"I don't know," he said. "That's never happened in all the time we've been friends. One of us *always* wins."

"Meaning one of you pulls out all the stops to best the other one?"

"Yeah," he said, remembering how Dirk caused him to lose the last no-sex bet.

"You've never compromised before?"

"No."

"I find that sad." Indeed, she looked quite forlorn.

Stunned, Tom simply peered at Jude as she dug in her purse for her door key.

She got the door opened and unlocked and stood to one side, her body language relaxed and inviting. "Well? Have you caught your breath yet?"

How could he tell her that the stairs had nothing to do with it, that she was the one who took his breath away?

"Are you ready to come inside where it's warm or is the allure of winning just too much for you to consider an alternative path?"

"Jude." Any residual air leaked from his lungs on that solo word.

"Come inside." She took him by the hand—he didn't resist—and led him into the foyer, closing the door behind them.

His heart thumped wildly in his chest as the moment unfolded. She moistened her lips. He lowered his head. She made a small helpless noise low in her throat.

Screw the bet.

He was out. O.U.T. He didn't care about his competition with Dirk anymore. Jude was all that mattered. His only goal was to make her happy.

Tom kissed her gently, drawing her tongue into

his mouth but dropping his hands, and he knew to the depths of his soul that this wasn't just sex.

It was—

Well, he didn't know what it was. Didn't know how to label it. But whatever was happening, he wanted it to go on and on forever.

The wildest and best sex he'd ever had was nothing compared to Jude's mouth on his. He ached to be inside her, but a warm, quiet joy beyond his experience overpowered him. He could hardly breathe; his knees were trembling.

The first time he'd run a four-minute mile, he'd had the flu. He'd been terrified every step, afraid he'd get sick in front of the crowd at the track meet, afraid he'd disgrace himself and fail his team. He'd exerted himself to the max, his feet sprouting wings because he was desperate. That race was nothing compared to the effort it took to pull away from Jude.

"I can't," he whispered.

"Forget the bet," she coaxed, running her tongue along his jaw, encouraging him to throw caution to the wind.

"This isn't about the bet."

"You sure about that?"

"This is about you and me." He paused. "Us."

"What about us?" She stiffened in his arms.

"It's too soon. We need time to get to know each other. I want to enjoy every second of this."

"So let's start now," she cooed, her wicked little tongue flicking his earlobe.

It took every ounce of willpower inside him, but he stepped away from her amazing mouth. "No."

"Why not?"

"You're too nice for this," he said.

"For what?"

"Meaningless sex."

"It would be meaningless to you?"

No, no, it wouldn't and that was the problem. "You think you want casual sex, but trust me, you don't. You're just not built that way, Jude."

"You don't get to make that decision."

"I can't stop you from having sex, but I *can* stop you from having sex with me."

"Be honest. You won't have scx with me because you care too much about winning." There was a tremor in her voice and her eyes looked stricken.

She was hurt.

He'd hurt her and it crushed him.

"Dirk is right. Winning is all you care about. You are who you are. You're a competitive guy. I can't change you. Honestly, I don't want to change you."

Clearing his throat, Tom said the truest thing he knew. "I do care about winning." He paused to laser his gaze straight through her. "I care about winning...*you*."

"I'm not a prize to be won," she said. "But this *is* my fault."

"How's that?"

She set her chin and held on to his gaze, a desperate light coming into her eyes. "I haven't been completely honest with you."

His chest tightened and he bit down on his bottom lip, suddenly filled with apprehension. "About what?"

"I was supposed to get you so turned on tonight that we either had sex or you went home and broke your vow of celibacy."

"Wait." Tom shook his head and frowned, confused. "What?"

"When Dirk and I went out the other night..." She stopped to inhale a huge breath. "He told me how damaging your competitive spirit had become to both of you."

"*My* competitive spirit?"

"He wants to stop the way you two try to outdo each other. He's over it. He's ready to grow up and leave the past in the past."

"And you believe him?"

"I do." Jude notched her chin upward and met his gaze, but she couldn't hold it for long. "He says your rivalry, which was fun in the beginning, has become toxic."

"Me? He's the one who made the damn bet!"

It took a moment for Tom to register what she said. She and Dirk were in cahoots? They'd been talking about him behind his back. No, not just talking about him, scheming against him.

"Dirk is sincere," she said. "He proposed the entire bet in order to show you how silly this competitiveness between you had gotten. He truly wants out."

"And that's why he recruited you into trying to get me to violate the terms of the wager."

"We did the same thing to him last night."

"I can't believe this. Dirk is manipulating you."

"No." She shook her head.

"Yes." He nodded fiercely. "You don't know what you're dealing with. Tell me *exactly* what Dirk told you."

"Honestly, by getting so agitated, you're proving his point." Jude pursed her lips.

"Of course I'm getting agitated. You were conspiring with my enemy."

She let out a long sigh and lightly scratched her temple. "It wasn't like that at all. Dirk was worried about you and asked me to help him help you."

Okay, he couldn't really get mad at her. She was naïve. Gullible. She didn't know Dirk the way he did.

"He's a puppet master. His goal is to win. Always and forever."

"Dirk said that you would say that."

"Can't you see how he's gotten you wrapped up in the competition?" Tom asked. "It's insidious. His need to win."

"And you don't have that same driving need?"

Tom couldn't say no to that. Once upon a time, he'd been as ruthless as Dirk. "How can I prove to you that I'm no longer interested in Dirk's stupid bet?"

She cast a glance at her bedroom door.

His heart was in his throat. "Are you suggesting—"

"Show me the truth of who you are at heart. Stay. Spend the night with me."

"No." He raised his hands and backed up toward the door. "This isn't you, Jude. Dirk has gotten into your head and convinced you to see things his way."

"Oh, Tom." She looked so incredibly sad, as if her heart were breaking. "Do you seriously think I would go to bed with you just to help Dirk win the competition?"

"That's not what I'm saying."

"What *are* you saying?"

"I'm saying you're too nice. You believe the best in people."

"You underestimate me, Brunswick." She sounded peeved. "You have two choices. Stay here with me tonight and tomorrow tell Dirk you're out of the competition. Or..."

Or?

Her eyes said it all. If he didn't walk away from the bet, it was as good as admitting he did have a problem with his competitive nature and that winning meant more to him than having a relationship with Jude.

But it was no longer about the bet. Jude had conspired with Dirk against him. That's what hurt. That's where the knife's blade cut deep.

In a daze, he grappled for the door handle.

"You're leaving?" Disappointment snatched her mouth downward.

"I have to. I can't—"

"Stand losing?"

He didn't even reply to that, just left her apartment at a dead run, taking the stairs two at a time until he reached the vestibule, and burst outside into cold air that beaded the sweat on his forehead.

Even though he'd never convince Jude otherwise, his running out on her had nothing to do with Dirk or the damnable bet.

He simply couldn't have a casual fling with Jude. She deserved better. He had to stop seeing her. His hormones—and his heart—were going haywire. If he could just have sex with her—get her out of his system, he would. But he could not. Something deep inside told him that if he ever made love to Jude, he could not just walk away unscathed.

He hopped into the Mustang, knowing he could have enticed her to do anything, everything. She wanted him as badly as he wanted her. He started the engine and backed up, afraid he'd shrivel up and die if he didn't make love to her.

It wasn't too late to go back.

He stopped at the ramp leading to the road, too shaken to drive and aching to return to her.

Just once. If he could make love to her just once, it might break the spell she had on him. He could get back to normal; he could feel like a separate individual again, his life unfettered by an overwhelming need for her.

But he knew that was a lie. If he had sex with Jude, he would never be the same again. Some truths were just too profound to escape.

Once wouldn't be enough, not with Jude. Not nearly enough. She'd gotten under his skin and into his heart. He wanted her in bed and out of it, but she was far too pure for him.

Now he understood why her fiancé had left her at the altar. It had nothing to do with Jude and everything to do with Jaxon's own inadequacies.

Inadequacies Tom shared.

And he just wasn't ready to face them yet.

❧ 14 ❧

Tom's Autumn Fling Sale was in full swing, and business was good enough to hire another part-time person. He even had a shop-late week, staying open until ten every night. He worked the extra hours himself, too tired to do anything but drop into bed at the end of fourteen-hour days.

It was better than moping around his apartment missing Jude.

He'd picked up the phone to call or text her a dozen times in the past two weeks, but what could he say? She believed he couldn't control his competitive nature, and he believed she was far too nice for a guy like him.

He'd be okay when the hollow ache went away.

Meanwhile, he couldn't risk seeing Jude again—or

even talking to her on the phone. He had the unfortunate habit, where she was concerned, of opening his mouth when his brain was on hold.

After he left Jude's house that night, Tom texted Dirk. U Win.

Dirk replied with a suitable amount of gloating and then invited Tom to play pool at The Loophole.

Tom did not go. In fact, he didn't even text Dirk back. Their relationship was nothing but an ongoing competition. Always had been and always would be if he decided to continue the friendship.

Which he was not inclined to do. He disliked how his buddy had used Jude, but he didn't even bother to tell Dirk that he knew what he'd done, recruiting Jude to help him win. The guy would stoop to anything for a score.

You're the same way.

No, he wasn't. Not anymore. Not since he'd met Jude.

Shaking his head, Tom returned to the task at hand, sanding a small computer desk a regular customer had commissioned for her daughter to use when she went off to college.

He was alone in the back of the store when the bell over the door jangled. Wiping his palms on the seat of his jeans, he sauntered into the main part of the store and saw his twin sister striding toward him.

Tara seemed to glow, and he had to admit, marriage agreed with her. Unlike his own dark hair, hers was newly highlighted with threads of gold. When he looked in the mirror, he saw lackluster brown eyes with fatigue shadows. Hers had sparkle.

"Hi, sis. You're lookin' good."

"Thank you," she beamed.

"Mom left early," he said. "She had an appointment with her CPA."

"I didn't come to see Mom."

"Huh."

"I've been in my honeymoon bubble, but I had to find out what's going on with you."

"Me? Nothing's going on with me."

"The aunties and Mom are worried. You haven't accepted any family invitations and you haven't been returning texts or calls." She wagged a finger. "I don't know what's happening with you—"

"It's called working hard."

"*Hmph*. That's an excuse." She tossed her head. "Anyway, the aunties are badgering me to find out if you're coming to Thanksgiving dinner or not. Since you didn't answer *my* texts either, I decided to check on you to see if you were still alive."

He shrugged, not bothering to argue with a woman who'd shared his bathwater more than a quarter century ago.

"The aunties also want to know if you're coming to Thanksgiving and will Jude be your plus one. By the way, dinner is at two p.m. and Pru says be on time or else!"

Aah, there it was. His family's motivation for sending Tara over here. To find out if he and Jude were still an item.

"I'll be at Thanksgiving..." He paused. "Without a plus one."

"Oh, really, Tom?" His sister looked practically heartbroken.

"It's fine."

"I really liked Jude. What did you do to send this one running for the hills?"

"That's none of your business."

"Ooh, little brother is getting pissy. You know I'm asking myself why."

He wasn't rising to the bait and telling her anything about Jude. "I'm only two minutes younger."

"And those two minutes make all the difference," she teased, and then her tone turned sympathetic. "It must have been a tough breakup if you're not willing to talk about it."

"We didn't break up. We were never together. You can't break up with someone you're not with."

"Jude might see things differently."

"What do you mean?" He scowled.

"For a smart guy, you sure can be dense some-times," she said and walked right out the door.

He hated that his twin always seemed to get the last word.

❧

TOM SHOWED UP AT AUNT PRU AND UNCLE Horace's house on Thanksgiving afternoon, promptly at two p.m. as instructed. The house was packed with relatives and it was easy—after the arrival hugs and greetings—to find a spot out of the fray.

He was sitting in the corner playing a game on his phone when the front door opened and two more guests were ushered in.

Dirk and his date...

Jude.

His college buddy had his arm draped around Jude's shoulders as if it belonged there.

Tom positioned himself out of their direct line of sight, then ducked his head and prayed they didn't see him. He was also trying to gauge if he could slip out the back door unnoticed and get the hell out of there. Considering the number of nephews engaged in horseplay between Tom and the door, he guessed his chances were slim to none.

One of his aunts ushered Dirk and Jude into the

kitchen to deposit the food they'd brought, and Tom took the opportunity to head upstairs.

At the top of the landing, he ran into his sister who was coming out of the restroom, readjusting her clothing. Her grinning new husband followed, zipping up his pants.

"At Aunt Pru's? For shame, sister." Tom shook his head.

"We're married." Tara jutted her triumphant chin in the air. "It's allowed."

"Maybe I should just ask Aunt Pru about that. Or Mom."

"No, don't!" Tara grabbed his arm.

"She talks a big game." Ben kissed the top of Tara's head. "But she's terrified of your mother and her sisters."

"Hell," Tom said. "I am too, but..." He pointed his index finger at his twin. "I have a bone to pick with you."

"Me?" Tara put a palm to her chest. "What did I do?"

"Why are Dirk and Tara standing in Aunt Pru's kitchen?"

She shrugged and raised both palms but couldn't meet his gaze. "I dunno. The aunties might have mentioned something about inviting Dirk, but I knew nothing about the Jude thing."

"They're pretty much a couple nowadays," Ben said, along with a soft *oof* as Tara nudged him in the ribs with her elbow.

Dirk with Jude? They were dating? Tom's stomach sickened. He'd shoved her right into Dirk's arms.

"We should go downstairs," Tara said.

"Are you going to punch Dirk?" Ben asked. "You look like you're going to punch him."

"I'm not going to punch him," Tom said.

"Why don't I believe you?" Tara canted her head and sized him up with a dramatic side-eye.

"Aunt Pru just texted," Ben said. "She wants everyone at the table. She's serving dinner now. Her text is in all caps, so I think she means business."

"Gotta go!" Tara trotted past him down the stairs.

"Don't worry." Ben clamped a hand on Tom's shoulder. "Watching them together—Jude and Dirk —I don't think the chemistry is right."

"You saw them together?"

Ben looked rueful.

"When?"

"Tara and I double-dated with them last night. We went to The Loophole."

"What!"

"I told Tara you'd be upset."

"Next you'll tell me their vibes don't vibrate." Tom scowled all the way to his cheeks.

"Your sister thinks Jude's pining over you."

"Really?" His heart lurched and suddenly he was as needy as a teenager with his first crush.

"Tara is pretty perceptive. Trust her instincts." Ben's cell phone dinged again. "Oops, I'm not gonna be the one to incur Aunt Pru's wrath. Dinner is on the table."

Ben zoomed away.

His brother-in-law was right. Time to face the music. Tom had created this mess and he was the only one who could fix it.

Hauling in a deep breath, Tom followed Ben into the dining room packed with people and the woman he couldn't get off his mind.

❧

JUDE'S HEART HAD SKIPPED A BEAT WHEN SHE'D first seen Tom. She must have been crazy to come to his aunt's Thanksgiving dinner, even with Tara and Dirk coaching her that it was the right thing to do.

She had her doubts.

Seeing him standing in the doorway, his stare fixed on her, sent Jude's heart shooting into her throat. It was horrible feeling like a lovestruck teenager, tormented by physical longing even in the midst of a crowd. She wanted to spend every waking and sleeping moment with Tom, but she didn't want to talk to him.

How could that be?

Coward!

She never should have come, but Dirk had been insistent that Thanksgiving dinner at Aunt Pru and Uncle Horace's house was the perfect place and time to tell Tom the truth.

Jude took a deep breath, then straightened her spine. She had to put the ball in his court again. If he let her go again, she'd have to stop yearning for him and move on.

But there was no way she could sit down to dinner with Tom across the table and eat a bite of food. Not until they'd straightened things out between them.

Tom was all the way across the room, although his eyes had never once left hers. She couldn't read his face. Had no idea what he was thinking. She hadn't heard a peep from him in two weeks.

He wore a white chambray shirt with sleeves rolled to his elbows and the top snaps open to reveal a sexy V and a thatch of silky brown hair. His jeans hugged his thighs and didn't do much to turn off her overly active imagination. He was the only man she knew who was X-rated in ordinary clothes.

Jude wasn't even aware that they were moving

toward each other, but suddenly they were in front of each other, the lively family members all around them.

"Hello," Tom said, his voice coming out a little ragged. "We need to talk."

"Yes," she said, her own voice none too stable. "Someplace private."

"The basement okay?"

"That'll do."

"Hurry back," Aunt Pru said. "We'll wait to carve the turkey."

"No, we won't," Uncle Horace added. "You take all the time you need. We have three microwaves that'll heat up any cold food nicely."

Jude looked over her shoulder at Dirk, giving him a thumbs-up. He nodded and waved her away.

Tom scowled and she had the crazy idea he would throw her over his shoulder and carry her out if she didn't hurry. The same way he'd carried her up three flights of stairs the last time she'd seen him.

Instead, he took her elbow and literally pulled her into the basement and locked the door behind them.

Her heart galloped.

He smiled for the first time a wicked grin that made her feel hot needles in her nether regions. For some reason she couldn't fathom, he seemed to be enjoying himself immensely.

"What is it?" she whispered.

The look he gave her could melt butter. "Jude, I've got a burning question I need an answer to."

"All right." She braced herself, unsure what he was going to ask.

"Are you and Dirk..." He gulped so hard his Adam's apple jerked. "Did he...win you?"

"*Win* me? I'm not a Kewpie doll prize on some carnival midway game, Tom."

"Are you with him?"

"Do you mean is Dirk still in the competition?"

"Yes," he whispered so softly she could hardly hear him.

"As far as *I* know he is."

"Does that mean—"

"I'm not dating Dirk, if that's what you're asking."

"You decided not to go wild after all?"

"I told you a long time ago, there was someone else I was interested in, not Dirk."

"Oh." Crestfallen, he jammed his fingers through his hair. "Am I too late?"

"For what, Tom? To *win* me? Yes, yes, you are."

His shoulders collapsed and his eyes filled with so much pain that Jude could see exactly how much he cared for her.

"You're too late," she went on. "Because you're already won me."

"I have?" Hope bounced across his face.

She pressed her palms together in front of her heart and grinned wide. "You charmed the pants off me, Tom Brunswick, even though you were in no position to take them off."

"I did?" Gratitude laced through his voice.

"I'd like to continue to explore our relationship and to learn and grow together as a couple," she murmured. "If that's something you're interested in."

"Jude," he said, "there's nothing I would love more. But what about Dirk? If you're not dating him, then why are you here with him? Why did you double-date with Tara and Ben?"

"To arrange this. Dirk truly is sincere about curtailing the competitions between you two. In fact, he's got a woman he's interested in and although he hasn't confessed to you yet, he's already lost the bet. You win."

"I don't care about the bet," Tom said breathlessly, his intense dark eyes burning holes through her. "All I care about is you."

"Then why did you run out on me the last night we were together? Why haven't you called or texted me in the past two weeks?"

"Why haven't *you* called or texted me?" he asked.

"You were the one who left. I was giving you space and time to figure things out."

"But not today?"

"No," she said. "Not today. I couldn't stay in suspended animation waiting for you to come to your senses. Because of your help, I've become bold enough to go after what I want. Cards on the table, Tom. I want a relationship with you, but if that's something you can't give me, I need to move on."

He dropped to one knee in front of her.

Jude's heart flew into her throat again and sang like a caged bird. He wasn't about to propose to her, was he? That would be moving just a little too fast. They still had so much to learn about each other before things went that far, but she was hopeful that this time, she'd backed the man.

She admired so much about him—his positivity, his family, his thirst for lifelong learning and constant improvement. Even his desire to win was a good quality as long as he learned not to take it too far. She had confidence it was a lesson he'd taken to heart. She didn't want to change him. Instead, she wanted to bring out the best in him the same way he brought out the best in her. She'd only known him for a little over two weeks, but he'd already helped her so much to overcome her fears and live life on her own terms. To stop letting other people's opinions matter so much.

"What on earth are you doing?" she squeaked, her knees trembling.

He looked up at her from where he was still kneeling, a sweet grin on his face, and said, "Your shoe is untied."

"Oh!" She laughed.

"There," he said and patted her shoe. "All tied up nicely."

"Nice shoes for a nice woman?"

Tom got to his feet. "Sweetheart, you are so much more than just nice. You're wicked smart and unselfish. You care about people and making the world a better place, and all I want to do is learn more and more about you. It's been so much fun peeling back the layers of your personality."

"I feel the same way about you." Her breath slipped from her lungs, soft and fluid, awash in the flow of life, in the pivotal turning point.

Smiling, Tom tugged her into his arms and kissed her until her body was tingling from head to toe from it.

That's when the lights went out.

And there, in the basement of his aunt and uncle's home, one bold woman made love to one competitive man, shattering his vow of celibacy, and it was glorious.

EPILOGUE

ne year later...

"WHAT DO YOU THINK?" TOM ASKED AS HE CARRIED Jude over the threshold of the honeymoon suite of their Paris hotel room near the Eiffel Tower.

Jude Brunswick barely registered the magnificent view from the large plate glass window overlooking the romantic city. She was too busy staring into the face of her new husband, and her heart filled with such utter bliss, she could hardly contain her joy.

The past year had been a whirlwind as they dated and got to know each other fully. As they shared secrets, went on daring adventures, and made wild, crazy love together, each day had been better than the last.

"It's wonderful." She wasn't talking about the room with its brocade drapes and white French provincial furniture or the monument outside or the champagne iced in a silver bucket at the foot of king-sized bed.

"Now, Mrs. Brunswick," he said, setting her down as the door closed behind them, "what would you like to do first?"

"When in France, do as the Parisians do."

He murmured something terribly romantic in French—they'd taken French lessons together before the wedding, and they'd learned enough to get by in the City of Lights. She loved how he loved to learn as she did.

"And that means?"

"Making love, mon cheri." The language sounded so erotic on his tongue. "But first, a wager."

"Not another competition." She groaned good-naturedly. Truth be told, she adored the way he turned everything into a fun game and yet, at the same time, he'd learned how not to take his competitive streak too far.

It was the best of both worlds.

"Oh, you're going to like this competition."

"I am?"

His eyes glistened with desire. "I propose we see just how many times we can make love in one night. I'm betting my reputation on three."

"Three?" Jude scoffed. "This is our honeymoon. We'll make love at least four times tonight."

"You have much more confidence in my prowess than I do."

"My confidence is in the sexy lingerie in my suitcase, buddy. You'll be putty in my hands."

"Either way," he said. "It's a win-win competition."

"It's already three p.m., we better make haste and get on it."

"C'mere." He pulled her into his strong arms and kissed her deeply, seriously, his fingers busy with the buttons on her white linen suit jacket. Under it she was wearing only a lacy bra, and he plucked at one cup until his fingers embraced the naked swell of her breast.

He discarded her bra as quickly as he did her jacket, and then he slid her short skirt down her legs. It was incredibly arousing to stand naked in the arms of her new husband in a suit.

"I love you," he murmured. "So very much. Since you came into my life, nothing has been the same and in the very best of ways."

"Ditto," she agreed. "I love you more than words."

"So let's dispense with the words."

"On board with that."

Laughing, he started doing something wonderful with his tongue, at the same time dropping his hands lower, fondling her bottom until she almost danced with eagerness. His tongue teased her nipple, and his hand slid between her legs, parting them...

"God, being with you is a thrill a minute."

"We're going to have so much fun tonight. We should put room service on speed dial."

Nothing would ever be as much fun as making love with Tom.

"Mrs. Brunswick." He murmured her name with awe as if it were a mystical incantation. "My wife, my love, my heart."

"Haven't you forgotten something?" She reached out and parted his shirt, opening buttons with fingers made deft by desire.

"On it, babe. I'll never let you down."

HE UNDRESSED QUICKLY, HIS BODY STILL A WONDER to her—firm and strong with beguiling soft spots and places she could touch to reduce him to frantic eagerness. She'd lost track of how many times he'd melded his body with hers, each time deepening her pleasure and stoking fires she never expected to be extinguished.

Tom pulled her onto the bed and kissed her until her lips were ringed with the pinkness of passion and her wonderful pinkish-brown nipples were hard. He never knew what to expect; one minute she had to be coaxed, pulling a sheet to her chin and making a game of his urgency; the next she reached out to him, more exciting and erotic than he'd ever dreamed possible. He regretted every single night of his life not spent making love to her.

He couldn't imagine life without her. She was gorgeous, sexy, alluring—and the nicest woman he'd ever met. He still got cold sweats when he realized how close he'd come to losing her. Knowing she was really his was like looking at the world with new eyes. Maybe his euphoria wouldn't last, but his love would. There was nothing he wanted more than to make her happy.

Naked on the bed together, he moved over her, satisfied for the moment to admire her exquisite beauty—the smoothness of her skin, the lushness of her breasts, her graceful limbs and sleek little belly. When he parted her legs, he wanted to howl with happiness at her response.

Being inside her was like nothing he'd ever experienced. One moment she seemed lost in sensations, the next she caressed his shaft or ran her nails lightly over his buttocks. With any other woman, these were only erotic tricks, but there was so much love in Jude's touch that he was humbled, grateful, and aroused more deeply than he'd ever dreamed possible.

"I love you." He couldn't say it enough, but when, sooner than he'd expected, her stunning climax triggered his own, he couldn't stop saying it.

"I love you. I love you. I love you."

He cradled her against his chest, drowsy but not wanting to sleep, knowing how little rest he needed to be ready to make love to her again.

The wonder of it was, what happened between them wasn't just sex or any of the other terms he'd been using most of his life. He could only call it making love because that was what it was.

Later, much later, they lay with their legs entwined, her hair dark and glossy on his chest and her hand resting lightly on his shoulder.

He lifted her hand and looked at the sparkling solitaire—one diamond to represent one lifelong marriage, she called it—and the simple gold band she'd chosen, both more modest than he'd been willing to give her but more beautiful on her small hand than he could have imagined.

She admired it for a moment, then raised her

head and smiled at him with heartwarming joy on her face and murmured, *Mrs. Tom Brunswick.*

"To think," she said. "This all started with a bet."

"Speaking of bets," he said. "If you aim on winning, maybe you should change into that sexy lingerie while I call for room service. Sustenance is in order."

As he watched his wife walk bare naked into the bathroom, Tom knew that while this was the absolutely best day of his life, there was so much more ahead of them.

Laughter, competition, boldness, learning. The possibilities were endless because of the love they shared.

Because at the heart of it all, their compatibility, their respect and admiration for each other, and their fun and playful spirits were what truly mattered most of all.

Love.

Pure and simple.

The answer was always love.

DEAR READER,

Readers are an author's life blood and the stories

couldn't happen without you. Thank you so much for reading!

If you enjoyed The Makeshift Groom, Pam and I would so appreciate a review. You have no idea how much it means to us. You are the best! Keep reading and being your awesome, unique self.

If you'd like to keep up with our latest releases, you can sign up for Lori's newsletter @ https://loriwilde.com/sign-up/.

To check out our other books, you can visit us on the web @ www.loriwilde.com.

Love and light,

Lori and Pam

ABOUT THE AUTHORS

Pam Andrews Hanson

Before teaming up with Lori Wilde, Pam Andrews Hanson co-wrote more than fifty novels with her mom, including romance and cozy mysteries. She is a former journalist and currently teaches freshmen composition in a university English department.

Lori Wilde

Lori Wilde is the New York Times, USA Today and Publishers' Weekly bestselling author of 90 works of romantic fiction.

Her books have been translated into 26 languages, with more than four million copies of her books sold worldwide.

Her breakout novel, *The First Love Cookie Club*, has been optioned for a TV movie as has her series, *Wedding Veil Wishes*.

Lori is a registered nurse with a BSN from Texas Christian University. She holds a certificate in forensics, and is also a certified yoga instructor.

A fifth generation Texan, Lori lives with her husband, Bill, in the Cutting Horse Capital of the World; where they run Epiphany Orchards, a writing/creativity retreat for the care and enrichment of the artistic soul.

WRONG WAY WEDDING SERIES

The Groom Wager

The DIY Groom

The Stand-In Groom

The Royal Groom

The Makeshift Groom

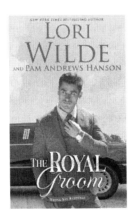

My other car is a limo.

Leigh Bailey returned the heavy gas pump hose and glimpsed the bumper sticker on her shabby little convertible. Rain blew in her face, obscuring her vision for a moment and taking away her breath.

Her chances of ever owning a limo on her salary were nil, but wouldn't it be nice to sit in a spacious back seat while a chauffeur braved the Florida storm to tank up for her?

Never mind that she shared the same last name as her wealthy cousins, *the* billionaire Baileys from Detroit. Her branch of the family was church mouse poor.

Well, a girl could dream, couldn't she? Meanwhile, she had a long trip ahead of her. She sprinted toward the convenience store, unsuccessfully dodging puddles.

The rain tried to follow her into the small building, adding to the water on the floor before she could shut the door. For a storm that was supposed to bypass Florida, Hurricane Jeff was delivering a deluge.

She stood for a moment, letting water run off her red nylon rain poncho, and brushed away the drops streaming down her forehead. Her car was less than twenty feet away at the pump, but she'd still gotten soaked.

In a hurry to be on her way before the storm worsened, she got in line behind a tall dark-haired man in a green jacket. By the time she located the right credit card in her oversized canvas shoulder bag, she realized he was reading, not paying for gas.

In fact, he was literally studying the front page of the *Insider,* one of the country's sleaziest tabloids.

"Excuse me," she said, stepping around him and catching a glimpse of his long, lean jaw and strong features— hardly the kind of profile she'd expect to see buried in a gossip rag.

He gave a small start and hastily shoved the copy of the *Insider* back on the rack, as though she'd caught him doing something dirty. Without meeting her gaze, he hurried over to the beverage case.

There was something unusual about the way he moved—a grace that was hard to define. She'd never seen anyone who looked less like a tabloid junkie, even though she hadn't had a good look at his face.

"The power of the fake news," she muttered under her breath, annoyed by her own curiosity. What was so interesting in the *Insider?*

She ignored the bored-looking boy waiting to take her card and quickly scanned the tabloid headlines. She didn't think it was the story on aliens landing in Ohio that had him so intrigued. It had to be the other page-one story: ***Soap Heiress Dumps Prince Max for Bullfighter.***

Darcy Wolridge shocked friends and family by eloping with the idol of the Spanish bullring, Jose Perez, amidst rumors she was number one on Prince Max's list of prospective brides.

The brokenhearted Maximilian of Schwanstein is believed to be in the U.S. shopping for a bride. Who will be the lucky lady now that lovely Darcy has shattered his hopes?

A huge grainy picture showed the heiress draped on the shoulder of a macho-looking guy in a snake-skin jacket. The article continued on page eleven, but Leigh had seen enough. Darcy and the prince had been an item for weeks in the fairy-tale world of the tabloids. Leigh didn't want to read some sappy fiction about Maximilian's broken heart.

Her article about the prince would be classy—if she could find him. And if he'd talk to her.

Her credentials from *Celebrity* magazine carried more weight than an *Insider* reporter's, but only because she worked for the hippest gossip magazine around. A magazine that served up content in print, online, and TV. Both magazines chased the rich, the famous, and the ridiculous, but Prince Max could change all that for her.

If she could convince him to give her a serious, insightful interview, it might be her ticket to a better job. She'd have a good chance at moving to *Issues*, owned by the same media conglomerate as *Celebrity,* but a world away in content. Their writers didn't ride in limos, either, but neither did they have to write about rock stars in rehab and supermodels' skin secrets.

First, she had to find the prince. All she had to go on was a tip from her uncle Paul Donovan in West Palm Beach. An avid stamp collector, he'd picked up a rumor on the internet that the prince might pay a visit to the president of the Schwanstein Stamp Collectors Society. Max would supposedly stay at a plush Paradise Beach hotel, and that was Leigh's destination. Her editor thought the lead was solid enough to authorize travel expenses.

Leigh hurried back to her car, trying to believe the weather report she'd heard just before leaving Miami, where she worked out of *Celebrity*'s East Coast office. But if this was only a rain squall, she was Lady Gaga.

Torrential rain, driven by the wind, blanketed the windshield and swept across the on-ramp with the force of a giant fire hose as she crept back onto the highway. She wanted to wait out the storm in some nice dry place, but the prince was notorious for keeping on the move.

"If you'll tell your real story to a sympathetic reporter," she said, rehearsing her appeal, "it might stifle some of the silly rumors."

She had a more immediate problem: the taillights ahead of her had vanished in a wall of water. She dropped her speed to a crawl, wondering whether it was worse to hit the car ahead or be rear-ended because she was going too slow.

Traffic was coming to a stop. Flashing red lights were visible through the downpour, and she realized cars were leaving the highway. A policeman in a tent-like slicker was waving everyone off to the right.

Never one to docilely obey, she rolled down her window far enough to shout at the cop.

"What's wrong, Officer?"

"Highway's flooded. Keep moving, please." He made an impatient gesture and looked as if he wanted to give her car a kick to get it going.

She complied. She was an intrepid reporter, not a fool.

Her sense of direction was about as reliable as the weather, so she followed the taillights ahead of her, hoping the driver knew an alternate route north. *She* certainly didn't, and she had no cell service for her GPS.

The cars gradually thinned out, making her wonder where all the highway traffic had gone. Apparently, this was an old state highway, neglected after the interstate was built. No traffic was visible in the oncoming lane, but she felt safer moving slowly through the downpour, not having to worry about passing.

Suddenly a great black shape streaked past her on the left, throwing up a ton of water. Her small car rocked sideways, and Leigh's heart did crazy flip-flops. She saw the aggressively bright taillights of the dark sedan as it cut in front of her, then her right front wheel skidded off the pavement onto the rain-softened dirt shoulder.

Made in the USA
Columbia, SC
16 October 2020